The Deliberate Truth

To Our Muses & Our Mothers

Order this book online at www.trafford.com
or email orders@trafford.com

Most Trafford titles are also available at major online book retailers.

Sharon Lannan, Shelle Cropper, Annie Howell-Adams, Joanna Brodziak.

Printed in the United States of America.

ISBN: 978-1-4269-7140-2

Trafford rev. 07/07/2011

PUBLISHING www.trafford.com

North America & international
toll-free: 1 888 232 4444 (USA & Canada)
phone: 250 383 6864 ♦ fax: 812 355 4082

The Deliberate Truth

Avery Adams & Andy Sontag

Contents

Of Blood & Brine

'Blessed is he that escapes the storm at sea,' but when the storm has formed internally, our sense of land is uneven. There are no safe ports to find shelter from the constant squall of young madness. Though, it is important to emphasize not just the follies, but the gift of all this chaos. When life clamps down with snarling jaws to shake and rattle like a violent tambourine, the only solace found is in the ride itself. It is sink or swim once the universe parts its folds and beckons the mind towards astral projections of the wild imagination and astonishing visions. We struggle to keep our heads above the avalanche of words and wars in the heart, but are rewarded in doing so, illuminating and banishing the ghosts that haunt the soul's attic. I say this as a declaration of reason and intention, in pursuit to give you scraps of insight into my tangled mind: to externalize all of this ever-blooming sensation has become a burden so immense, that I am poised with the ultimatum of writing my way out of from these fast-closing walls.

I digress to the blood of this particular account, which was documented through strange and wild eyes. My veins have boiled in the fires of the most ineffable ardor, and just as prominently have been knotted by sickening doubt and discord. Running through them is brine caked with salt. These pages were delivered by oceanic extremities, thoughts consigned to intransience by the cry of the mind's ebbing tide. Born to fisherman who toiled the gray seas, I understood that we are poised only with the option of groping into the ether of the experiment we know as human life with patient will and open heart. Armed with unceasing and unquenchable desire to experience this fantastical circus, this maddening and surreally wondrous world of which we reside.

Though blood cannot be mentioned without noting the integral heart, fueling the machinery of bone and flesh, which feels more than it could ever be expected to burden. The heart, of which without these pages would be trivialized by the lack of proper emotion. The heart that has tried to open its orifices to the sweetest touches, but still endures alien aches like a phantom limb even when it finds rhythmic beat in another. The heart that has tried mightily despite it's falls into solitude, searching for muses in a demonstration of the eternal crux of human emotion; a vessel that claws to survive until full.

Lastly, I reside to the bones of this hive of scrambled and anxious thoughts. The skeleton that aches for a life far from the skin it is bound to, dreaming of narrow streets, rich fields, distant oceans, restless with its resignation to mutualism and shared inhabitance with the labored heart and wandering mind. The bones that carry with them a desire to be more than just the framework, but to hoist this whole body of words as far as a passionate whisper could conceivably travel, and then a footstep further, out to the precipice between the beautiful and most horrifying, where the soul dangles it's toes over the edge. The hardened bones that endure because a story will remain tepid and limp, a flimsy orgy of words without its spine bracing it to be expelled beyond it's original flesh of crumpled, ink-stained volumes.

It has taken the immensity of the world pressing down upon me to squeeze out an acceptable dedication to the majesty of verdant life and brilliant love, to properly enunciate the magnitude of this cacophonous chaos and deduce the fateful shifting of the universe. I am no more enlightened than any other person, and in this I am steadfast, but I have felt nothing more excruciatingly in my heart and mind, blood and bones than the vivid, salty brine of existence coursing through me, desperate for a page or an ear, and inherently I must free it before it swallows me whole in its ability to conjure the vast sensation of feeling so ubiquitously. The storm is still brewing and the tempest will only be quelled with a pen, so I scrape onward at the glacial surface that prohibits the kindling of understanding in the perpetual darkness of being. In this, the writer endures the most important struggle of all: to articulate the unknowable.

Street Ballet

It just started with a tap tapping. Feet moving on the floor, impatient audible grumbles.Then the overture, babies gasping for attention, yesterday's crinkling news, chatter humming like a street light on an empty lane. "Next!" Shouts the conductor, urging the dancers to shake in a caterpillar-like shutter, winding through the sectioned lines.The screeching, rusted shopping cart wheels of the brass section kick in and that's when I'm really moved by the whole composition.

People add their own bits too. One man rambling about buses or work or the woodwinds howling in from the cold outside. A woman shakes her cell from her pocket, answering a cappella, filling in the vacant notes with her clanking purse.

I try to get involved, moving at my own rhythm.Putting my hands in and out of my pockets, adjusting my hat, flipping open my cell phone. Nervous tics of the nervous mind.My cadenza is ridded with anxiety, but I try to play my part.

Everyone in the line seems to be dancing.Some steps are flat, but the music's really going now, and it's hard to resist. I keep thinking about my own moves, dancing around sanity, through the streets of this town. The people in front and behind have their own routines, I'm sure. I don't know much about them but I just try to step in sync. The crowds really finding the groove. The harmonies are tight, and the mass starts to shift in cut time.

The audience outside twists, shouts, and waits for a taste of the music coming from within. Buses blow by, filling out the low end. The older woman bobs her head in and out of the door like slow jazz.The streetlights beep out in falsetto, bringing more towards the concert, swinging through the painted white lines.

I'm up next at this big square dance, and I pass from my partners behind and move up to the prima at the window.She gives me the ok and I'm tossed into a full on pirouette, extra cards in hand because I brought my own bag. Now I'm in the band, contributing to the racket.

The percussion starts to roll. Cans clank, pasta shakes, and my feet get locked up in the back and forth of an awkward tango. The dancers ahead want to lead, but I keep hurrying the steps, because I've got places to be.I keep snapping my gum staccato, because the ugly nicotine banshee has raised her hideous head. The beat goes on.

Plucking away at the shelves, like strings to a harp, moving in time with the conductor's instructions. The whole sequence is really reaching the crescendo now. I'm antsy, all hands as I grope out for anything to hold onto.The music has taken me completely, and I'm just grabbing for items out of the arrangement to cook up later.

And all of a sudden the piece is over, and I'm spit out, dizzy and twirling like I'm still drunk. The band has other numbers, stirring undoubtedly, but I'm finding steps in the rain's slow nocturne. My sluggish waltz takes me to fourth where the movement's all interpretive. Everyone's got their own delivery and poise, and some dance in groups, while others need their own space to really shake it out.

I want to move slow, not just because my back's weighed down with food, but because the sounds are plentiful here. All these different cadences and rhythms keep the days on the balls of their feet, shuffling through down town.

In the cafes and diners, there are all sorts of choreography. It's all exits and entrances though. Dancers in from the door, stage left, while the waitresses dip for coffee, tips sometimes too. Some folks are participants, getting up from their seats, moving around, changing partners with a friendly exchange of words. Others linger in the audience commenting on the show, speculating, considering jumping in like an old-fashion swing dance.In the back, things are a bit more primal. Knives and pans, colliding in cannonball chorus. The cooks grind away. Their moves aren't flashy, but they step with confidence and deliberate purpose. The food can't stay still either. It's a sloppy dance, and most of the movements are guided by hands, to plates, to mouths. A tragic swan song.

One foot follows the other. Ears looking for music. The scene scored by the crackling of tobacco turning to smoke and ash, into the lungs, breathed out into vacant air waiting to be filled with noise.

Then to the bus where everything finds the beat again. The recorded voice that sways down from the sky, lines the walls, calls out dance steps. dictates agendas. Everything's in sync, starting on the one count, stopping, moving again, boarding and departing. Silently, I wonder if we can call it dancing: sitting motionless while in motion?

By the time I'm home, all that's left is just the tap tapping. My sneakers against wet concrete squeak with treble, while my beating heart carries the rhythm, hard in my chest, because I'm out of shape and smoke too much. The dance has left me, but I still feel all the music in my bones. My guts full of noise like a hive of entranced wasps. This town manages to keep hips swinging. It creaks and groans, and jangles like a ghostly tambourine. Sometimes the music is hidden, but I still find myself shaking down to electric 4th avenue, amongst swaying buildings, because the city pulses and shakes constantly, and I feel it vibrating in my veins. Tap, tap, tap.

Gospel

I don't want to talk about angels, because the only difference I see between us is a set of wings and golden rings above their fragile heads. As they manifest tableaus of rapture, visions of faith, gold meadows and green pastures, pearl gates lining the clouds, they conjure images of death, bronze bells blaring out one great cacophonous and ceremonial holy hallelujah from the skies above.

And I certainly don't want to touch on divinity, because we're all under impermanence's thumb. Our constructed ideas of a bearded man hanging on cedar planks for every time we fucked up, shadowed by his omnipotent father judging all, can't outlast the crushing weight of passing time. There's no merit in putting on your Sunday best anymore. In this delusional age, there aren't commodities of faith worth hocking to the masses, and the only things we can ever really count on are our friends. In a decaying day, surely it seems they have graduated to sainthood.

While it's convincingly true that anything worth wanting is satisfactory to obtain, the radio pantheon preaches, "You can't always get what you want." There may be salvation in a long night of drinking and dancing, but if I could see all my friends tonight, I might cry to the sound of our young gospel and my heart might fall out of my chest and spill all over these pages. My friends have got demons at their doors too. Everyone is selfish when their back's against the wall.

Like poor Christian. Named in holiness? Holy Chris. Saintly Chris, musing over missing pieces. Poor Chris, humbled by Life's immensity. You can imagine it though: new house, new town, old habits, only culminating in a punched drivers license and a court date in November. He can play Dillinger all he wants, cornered into well-rehearsed escapism, but an old, worn collection of short stories tells us that we'll be judged for our sins in the end. He's more fragile now than ever. We all are, to a certain extent, and his wounded heart will stay sick and broken for now, because we've fully accepted self-destruction as release.

Chris knows something that I didn't for many years. He says that all our spools unwound eventually, and instead of keeping yourself drunk on the communion wine, you gotta live for yourself, like it was born in your blood. You gotta rise up out of the catacomb slums of disillusion like Excalibur being pried out of the stone. We've all got expiration dates tattooed across our necks, God too, so we better walk onward like the universe was at our side, taking notes with a pad and pen.

Chris might have devils deep down, but he's flesh and blood and bones like you and I. He knows what love is, knows what he wants - which is more than most have. Despite the cracks in his carapace, he has the heart to rattle the stars like the cannon balls and pipe bombs of holy war, fervor of howling dogs, and an armada of words to say with, not necessarily what is right, but what he feels he needs to. And if anyone is entitled to vomit out notions of some holy truth, than he can surely speak in self-interest.

So count your angels. Sing your saints. Indulge your demons. Know your sins like you know your friends, because they manage under everyone's skin, and must be respected, held close. Get those hands in the thick batter of life, because although there might be a pair of ever-vigilant, spectacled eyes above, the only judges and juries I know are simply judges and juries. Please, allow me to testify: life is short, love is sweet, and either we will die or the world before us. Either way it will all fade into impermanence. Amen.

Eremophobia

Alex wakes up at 7:04 to the sound of a buzzing alarm clock. Alex is running late. Alex is reluctant to get out of bed, because it's very cold in his apartment. Alex begrudgingly gets out of bed.

Alex stumbles into the bathroom and tries to piss but gets his urine partially in the toilet and partially on the seat because he has a hard on. Alex cleans up the toilet. Alex looks in the mirror and decides not to shave today, because he does not give a shit. Alex gets in the shower.

Alex takes a fish oil pill, a zinc pill, a vitamin c pill, and a vitamin a pill. Alex takes these every day. Alex eats a calcium chew last because he thinks they're tasty. More over, Alex knows that the chew will be one of a short list of highlights in his day.

Alex feeds his dog, Ernest, and gives him fresh water. Alex loves Ernest. Ernest does not know his head from his asshole, because he is a dog, but it's safe to say that he loves Alex.

Alex makes toast and watches his coffee pot fill. Alex fills his thermos with coffee, butters his toast, says good-bye to Ernest, and walks out the door. Alex is in a hurry.

Alex starts his car and backs out of his driveway. Alex shuffles through the radio stations hoping to find some music that he likes. Alex cannot find anything worth listening. Alex keeps driving.

Alex has to stop the car at a red light shortly after exiting the free way. Alex is anxious and thinks that he does not have time for this shit. Alex sips at his coffee.

While Alex waits, he remembers that he needs to call Ms. D, his landlord. Ms. D has left several messages on Alex's phone because he is late on the rent. Alex has been ignoring her calls. Alex is getting paid today and will surely square up with Ms. D. Alex was late on the rent because he had to take Ernest to the veterinarian. Ernest is doing better. Alex loves Ernest. Ms. D couldn't give a fuck.

Alex takes the same elevator to the same floor and sits at the same desk doing the same menial tasks everyday. Alex does not like his job. In fact, Alex hates his job more than anything in the world.

Alex works at an insurance firm, which he jokes has firmly insured the likelihood of him blowing his brains out. Alex doesn't say this often because he knows that more and more often he isn't joking. Alex takes a deep breath.

Alex's boss, Doug Dexter is not a good person. Doug Dexter is an alcoholic, an abusive husband, a neglectful father of two, and a tyrannical employer who finds great amusement in belittling his workers. Alex cannot fathom how a man like this found himself in any sort of position of power. Alex remembers that Dick Cheney was in the White House for eight years and understands.

Doug Dexter spends the morning walking from desk to desk, making sure his workers are maintaining productivity. Alex wishes that he would stop circling around the desks like a vulture and let everyone do their work. Alex is on edge.

Alex tries to work but he is distracted. Alex can't seem to focus, so he goes outside for a cigarette. Alex has recently started smoking again. Alex knows it isn't healthy, but it keeps him sane. Alex tries to delay going back to work for as long as possible. Alex wonders what Ernest is doing. Ernest is at home, licking his balls.

Doug Dexter has a hangover and is not in the mood for any fun and games. Alex is not aware of Doug Dexter's current state, and takes his sweet time. Doug Dexter notices that Alex is lollygagging. Alex is oblivious. Doug Dexter is angry.

Doug Dexter approaches Alex, walking quickly, looking decidedly pissed. Alex is reclining in his chair, playing solitaire. Alex jumps when Doug Dexter yells his name.

Doug Dexter shouts, "What do you think you're doing!? Wasting mine and the company's time?" Doug Dexter tells him that his on thin ice; that he has been slacking for weeks and that there are a million other people in this godforsaken town who'd be happy to take his job. Doug Dexter asks what he has to say for himself. Alex has no excuse. Alex says nothing, and stares back blankly. Doug Dexter is greatly displeased. Doug Dexter has reached his final straw with Alex and points to the door. Alex tries to argue. Doug Dexter gets only angrier, his finger still directing Alex to the exit. Alex doesn't think his day can get worse. Alex does not yet know that it surely does.

Ms. D is an impatient woman, a woman who does not care for excuses, or children, or pleasantries, or dogs like Ernest. Ernest is only a dog, but if he knew this, he would surely be sad. Ms. D really only cares for money and Morgan Freeman.

Alex, now fired from his job has neither money nor Mr. Freeman's number, and is now exclusively an inconvenience to Ms. D. Alex knows that he is fucked.

Ms. D leaves Alex a message explaining that if the rent was not in her hands by five o' clock she would evict him. Alex lights a cigarette. Ms. D thinks Alex is avoiding her calls, accepting the fact that his likelihood as a continued tenant was slim. Ms. D puts an ad on Craigslist.

Alex, driving and smoking, notices that he has a call from a number that he does not see often. Alex doesn't talk about it much, but he has a son. Alex's son's name is Charlie. Charlie is six years old and gets to visit his dad for two months in the summer and over Christmas. Alex loves Charlie, but Charlie's mother does not care much for Alex, nor does she think that he is capable to raise a child. Charlie's mother is probably right.

Sheila, Charlie's mother, lives two states away and works at her sister's salon. Sheila is a complicated individual, who believes that her problems stem from the men in her life (her father, Alex) and can be fixed with prescription pills. Sheila also thinks that the public education system is failing and that Charlie needs to be academically challenged at a higher quality, private elementary school. Charley is six. Sheila lives in a delusional reality.

Alex is legally obligated to help Sheila pay for Charlie's schooling. Alex has repeatedly argued that there is no reason for a six year old to attend a private school. Charlie does not know any better, but he likes his school, because they have juice in the morning. Charlie really likes juice.

Sheila has called Alex on this particular day because Charlie's tuition is due next month. Sheila doesn't know about Alex's mishaps with Ms. D or Doug Dexter or Ernest recent illness, but it can be safely assumed that she couldn't give a rat's ass.

Sheila has squandered much of her money on needless therapy sessions and on refilling her prescriptions.Alex knows Sheila is calling about money as soon as he reads her number on his phone. Alex hesitantly calls back.

Sheila answers rudely. Alex is subservient and is easily intimidated by Sheila, but tries to make pleasantries. Sheila does not care for this, and launches into a full explanation of what a loser she thinks Alex is and how he better have money for Charlie's tuition. Alex does not have the money, and is not as much of a loser as Sheila thinks, but his current circumstances certainly make a strong case.

Alex tells Sheila about Ms. D and Doug Dexter and Ernest, but is met with a volley of shouts over the phone. Alex is stressed out. Sheila tells him that he better get his act together or he will loose all custody of Charlie. Alex doesn't know what to say. Alex can feel the world crashing all around him. Sheila hangs up. Alex hangs his head.

Alex is driving quickly and purposefully, tears running down his face. Alex's throat is dry and raspy from smoking almost an entire pack of cigarettes. Ernest is expecting to be home soon and is getting antsy. Alex doesn't make it home in time to take Ernest for his usual walk at six. Alex has pulled into Wal-Mart.

A ex walks through the aisles quickly. Alex's hands are sweaty and shaking. Alex walks up to the man behind the counter in the back and points and what's he wants. Alex shows the man some paperwork that has been useless to Alex until today. Alex pays and walks back to his car.

Alex's eyes are swollen from tears. Alex drives to the park where he and Sheila had their first date. Alex still loves Sheila. Sheila left Alex for someone else, but Alex still loves her. Alex doesn't even want an apology. Alex just wants his family back.

Alex sends Sheila a text message that reads, "I'm sorry." Alex opens up the case to his newly purchased semi-automatic hand gun. Alex's tears are hot on his face. Alex loads a bullet into the chamber and releases the safety. Alex's hands are shaking terribly. Alex tries to think, to look back on his life, but nothing comes. Alex strains as hard as he can to search through the old tombs of his dreary life for any sign of relief but can only feel his temples throbbing behind his closed eyes and heart beating hard in his chest. Alex sticks the cold metal barrel in his mouth. Alex's teeth wrap around boxy, metallic shaft of the hand gun and he weeps and weeps.

Alex's finger is dancing around the trigger. Alex wants to pull it. Alex wants to end it all. Alex wants to run the fuck away and never come back. Alex hears a beep coming from his glove compartment. Alex returns to the trigger, but the beeping continues. Alex is furious because he knows that he cannot pull the trigger with that awful blaring alarm.

Alex opens the glove compartment and out fell a slew of papers along with his beeping watch. Alex grabs one paper in particular. Charlie likes to draw and send his dad stories he wrote. Charlie loves Ernest, and likes to draw him in particular. Alex starts to sob even harder. Alex still has the gun in his hand.

Alex is trying to focus hard now. Alex sticks the gun between his eyes and closes both of them. Alex, through shaking breathes looks back up at the gun. Alex stares into the barrel. Alex's hands are sweating and he can barely grip the gun. Alex is light headed. Alex's mind drifts from face to face, slipping through memories. Sheila is in the park, wearing a dress, hair down. Charlie is learning to walk and eating apple sauce. Ernest is getting older but still sits by the bed. Ms. D is making her famous casserole. Doug Dexter buys his wife flowers and tells her he's going to try harder. Alex doesn't think he can cry any harder but the tears somehow find a way to fall. Alex rolls down the window and hurls the gun into the creak by the park. Alex starts the car and drives as fast as he can towards home. Ernest is at the door. Alex can see him as he gets closer. Alex does not want to run away. Alex cannot run away, because he has reasons to wake up the morning. Alex loves Sheila. Alex loves Charlie. Alex loves Ernest. Alex will not give in today.

Muted

Once I had gotten off the bus I knew that the only things left in my bank account were mistakes and bad impulses. In my blistering life I had inherited a trust fund of words, and their worth weighed heavy on me, especially then.

This particular city wasn't of much importance at the time. I was more concerned with the girl that had brought me to it. My relations to her had robbed me of any value in aesthetics or self-worth and wanted to spend the last of my words on her, for closure, if anything.

I walked down the thin streets, wind in my jacket, cigarette smoke sweeping in and out of my lungs like pendulum chimneys. Calm had washed over the town, marinating in a dull hush. I wondered how I was to find a girl in a big town wrapped up in all sorts of silence.

There were no alibis for my presence in this static city. I had used an entire canon of verbs and nouns, slanted diction, and a vicious syntactical delivery to mess things up in my life, and managed to continue to make them worse. I felt compelled though, by the immensity of my heart that I had to make things right between us. She had left early with the sunrise, and I knew she wasn't coming back unless I made the effort to fix what I had surely broken.

I hadn't drunk coffee in a couple months. It made me jittery, made me shit, messed with my sleep, and despite what people say, never helped with my hangover. But this town deserved a cup, I decided. It's quiet charm and cold wind deserved further atmospheric additions. I scanned the streets like an eight year old scours its word search for crumbs and clues. All the buildings, though unique in design and decoration, were nondescript. Curiously, there were no signs on any of the stores. No titles. No words directing anything here or there. Just silent concrete and somber brick lining the roads.

I moved along the streets, looking for any sort of discernible characteristics amongst the sprawling sea of faceless buildings. I was taken by the stillness of the entire city. There were no murmurs of life bouncing through the streets. Parked cars ran up and down blocks, but I got the impression that they were there permanently. I saw people walking beside the stores in silence, each step performed with the precision of a tightrope walker, carefully stepping with deliberateness, avoiding cracks, as to not make a sound as they went. I was floored by my observation that it appeared as though was as if the entire city was on mute.

The wind began to pick up, and I ducked in what I assumed was a small cafe. Scattered people sat in dim light, stirring at lifeless plates of food.I approached the counter, trying to get something to eat. The walls above the register had photographs of food, bowls of pasta, sandwiches, soups, and salads. The woman at the register approached me, staring me directly in the eyes. I don't particularly care for direct eye contact, because I am shy and tend to star off towards the ceiling. He gaze remained unflinching.

"Hi. Do you have a menu?" I asked. As if I hadn't said anything at all, the woman continued to stare directly back at me, eyes now wider than before, head cocked to the side. "Sorry, maybe I wasn't –"I cut myself off, as I turned around to see that everyone in the café was staring at me. I turned around to see the woman with her index finger raised over her lips. She then silently pointed up to the food. I whispered, "Why do I need to be quiet?"But as soon as the words left my mouth, a tall mustached man grabbed me by the lapel and pushed me towards the door. He made the same gesture over his mouth and gently closed the door behind him. I was frankly too confused to storm back into the café. What was the meaning of all this? I walked onward towards the city central.

The bus driver had told me to walk down Thomas Street to get to a beautiful park. But all the streets had either no name or were something nondescript like 'This Street' or 'That Street.' I pulled out my cell phone to check the time, and more importantly to call her, but there was no reception in this town.I puzzled over how I would find a girl in this seemingly lifeless void.

As I strolled up and down the dark, cobbled back streets of the city my eyes darted from block to block, looking for signs of her presence. Her halo of beautiful blonde hair. Her long, endless legs, soft lips, rosy cheeks. I stopped, sighing. She was everything to me still. There were no words to explain her beauty.

I found the city square by nightfall. Despite my confusion navigating the city, it was as though I had been intuitively drawn towards its center. This magnetism was apparent in the center's extreme beauty. Roses lined the square, and an elegant fountain rested in the middle, the rush of water cutting through the silence of dark. The street lights cast a blue glow over the walk way. She was there by the fountain, sitting motionless, as though she'd resided there for eternity, seemingly just another part of the beautiful square.

I walked slowly. Gripped with nerves, I realized I hadn't prepared anything to say, so I quickly rehearsed lines in my head. She was staring down the lonely streets, unaware of my approaching presence. I walked closer and called out.

"Sylvia, I'm so sorry," I told her, but like the woman in the café, the words I spoke seemed to sail over her. She gazed at me, eyes full of complex emotion. "Sylvia, please. Speak with me.I had no intention of hurting you. I love you."

The silence was agonizing. Finally looking up at me, I felt my breath catch in my chest. Her bright blue eyes, like robins eggs, stared nearly through me. They were bulging with sadness and longing. She turned back to the streets, and then abruptly stood up. She grabbed my hand, pulling me back towards the city

"Where are we going?" I asked her, met again with silence. We walked onward through the city. As we passed This Street and That Street again and again, I noticed a great glow coming form up ahead. The buildings were illuminated with warm light, and a great vibration rumbled from the streets ahead.

Around a corner, past another line of anonymous buildings I saw it. A great mass of a building, glowing radiantly, buzzing like chatter on a train. I listened closer and realized that it was actual voices oozing out to the streets. It was as if this great building was a giant hive of spoken words.I stared on in awe, but was dragged closer by Sylvia.

"Are we going in?" I asked. She pulled me onward.

It was like a million voices at once, chatting, yammering, howling, whispering. A great cacophonous orchestra of conversation and scattered thoughts reverberating around us. The walls of the building at first glance looked like static, the salt and pepper low of a television. Upon closer inspection, I saw that they were words scrolling across the walls. Single words, whole phrases, meandering thoughts, and audible blips racing around the room.It was magnificent. I shook in my shoes.

I was so taken by the whole building that I had barely noticed that Sy via had walked to another part of the room, and was carefully studying the passing words. Like a lion pouncing on it's prey she suddenly shot her arm out, grabbing at the wall. With a great peeling sound, she pried off a series of words, holding them tightly as they squirmed in her hands. She forcibly crumbled them up, grinding them nto fine powder. She smiled and then blew it towards me.

I was suddenly enveloped in memory. Regrettable words exchanged in the laundry mat. Plates, broken on birthdays. Wrong names accidentally whispered over pillows. The times when my words, despite my great affection for them, had betrayed me.

Vision returned to reality, Sy via smiling on. She looked at me again with those brilliant eyes and said, "These are the words we never meant to say. This is where they've come to rest. Floating out amongst all this chaos. Don't you see? I had to come here. I had to get rid of them, to make this right between us. refuse to cry over spilt milk. I refuse to let your loose tongue drag out love into insignificance."

" I don't understand. What is all this? This city? What is this place? Please explain, Sylvia," I pleaded.

"There are something's that don't need to be explained. There are something that just don't need to be said at all. You always got so tied up in saying the right thing or having something clever or charming to speak of.They're just words. Sometimes a moment merits silence, and that what makes it beautiful, or poetic. Sometimes I don't need to hear you say that you love me, because I just know it by the way you're eyes crinkle when you're tired, or when you count the freckles on my shoulders with you're fingers. "

"I do love you," I told her.

"I know. That's why you're here, why you even made the effort. It's why we fight and cry, and have sleepless nights. But, it's the very same reason why we can feel life coursing through us when we wake up in the morning next to one another," she smiled.

"Sylvia," I started.

"Don't. Not a word," putting a finger over my lips, than replacing it with her own, soft and sweet. We held each other for a moment longer, than left in silence.

I bare the burden of having too much to say, and my words seep out forcefully and consistently. I have subscribed to the theory that the complexities of life can be coaxed into understandable increments through the treatment of language. On this particular day I had a myriad of apologies and regrets heavy on my tongue, but sometimes silence, as anxious as it can make anyone, is the truest score of comfort and remorse. Sometimes the most deafening cries for forgiveness are made by a brush on the cheek, or a flash of a smile, and ultimately our actions are the supreme tell in the poker game of romance, and the simplest touch makes us willing to bet it all on love. I had come to this city running through all the right lines, all the right words, but what do you say to the girl who never fails to leave you speechless?

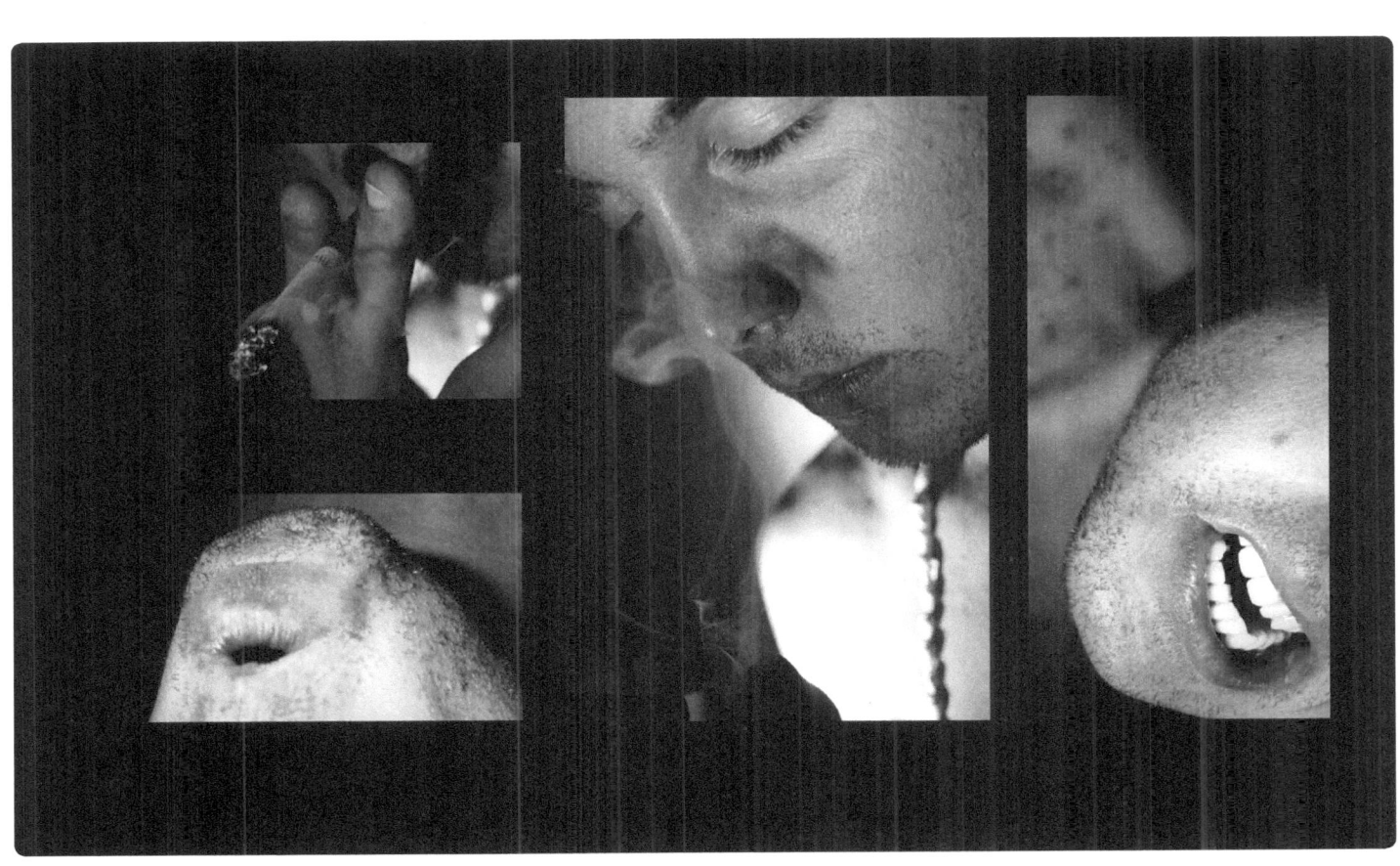

My Life With the Rat

My life with the rat began like my life with most things, inconsequentially. I saw it briefly in the garage. It saw me. It acknowledged my presence by scampering off behind the water heater into the guts of the house, probably a crawl space or hole gnawed through from the outside.Lighting my cigarette I wondered how it had found residence in our quiet abode, though I did not spend much time on it's recent arrival as the world was spinning madly onward, and there were things of much greater concern and corollary at the time.

I remained unmoved by my new rodent acquaintances' arrival until two nights later. I had seen it in the garage once again, still scampering at any potentially predatory racket. Causing enough of a startle each time I saw it for me to inform my roommates. Considering getting some traps, but again, not putting too much thought into it. Other things were going on: work, finals, but all of the mental clutter created by preoccupation was rudely interrupted at around two in the morning.

The gnawing was close to my head. I thought it to be a rude dream – a late night auditory hallucination. Scratching, persistent, unholy chewing at the carpet below the door to the garage. Wood splintered by ever-hungry jaws. Ravenous and insatiable, fevered by mindless animal drive. With only a thin wall separating my once sweet sleep and the frenzied assault on the wall paneling and carpet, I cringed in horror.

Reluctant and drowsy, I hosted my weary bones out of bed, muttering about working in the morning. Pausing at the door, irrational fear began to spread through me. Worries of getting bitten, getting the plague even, surged in my conscious. Only children bear the burden of the most wild of imaginations which in many cases is truly a gift, but often inspires the most terrible and irrational fears. The terror I experienced seems unreasonable in hindsight, but was excruciatingly real as I sat poised by the door. I grabbed a stick that leaned by the window, and with weapon in hand I jolted the door and flipped the light. Nothing.

I was sure of what I had heard, sure of the culprit. But alas, the whispers of the pest where only ghosts in the early morning. Scanning the kitchen, still without rodent traces. Back in bed I prayed for easy rest.

It went on like this for some while. Signs of the house's new resident rattled through the hallways on exact and repetitious cue each night at around one in the morning. Unlike a child's tantrum or flooding toilet, I felt that it cidn't demand immediate attention, and as I repeatedly returned to bed, sandwiching my head between two pillows, believing that like a pimple, this problem would go away if left alone.

The sound of instinctual rodent craving is as penetrating as the smell of death. It is not like white noise oozing out of the static television set, constant and droll. The rat has spine and beating heart pumping warm blood through its persistent veins.It will gnaw because it has to, like the junkie fighting to be clean, staring down a shot; it will act out of habit far beyond its limited consciousness. It faces the evolutionary battle of not the desire, but the compulsory need of mastication. Otherwise its teeth will grow clear out of its horrible jaws. As it chews, it gets tired like any other warm-blooded mammal. Its dental care is performed in bursts, a punctuated assault, a brief rest, then again, continually through the night. It is this routine that drove me to such madness.

Like the snooze button of cellular phone's alarm clock, the rat's waves of chewing was enough for me to feel the warm arms of sleep crawling over me before a sensation similar to that of a thumbtack scratching at my inner ear was ringing through my mind. I tossed and turned. Obligations in the morning were imminent, quickly approaching in the wee hours, stress and frustration pounding against my fragile brain. I continued to madly thrash with my covers. Enter delirium.

My eyes had swollen with the early morning, and I returned to the door leading to the garage hallway.Calling for my roommate, we both simultaneously peered out from our doors searching for the rat. We started back to one another, defeat and frustration sagging off our tired faces. I banged against the wall near the garage door, while he checked the kitchen to no avail. Upon returning to my bed I finally found some much needed sleep waiting for me.

The next night the circus routine continued. One o'clock: the overture, tentative and curious scratching. By two it was an unapologetic feast upon the carpet below the door. I could hear each individual strand of cotton fiber tearing from the wood paneling beneath it. With each tug, separating strand from the glue that held it down, a cringe coursed through me. I got up to check for the rat, stick in hand – looking to whack it good this time – again, nothing. Back under covers I envisioned the joy I would experience upon sleeping solidly through an entire night, cursing the phantom haunting the hallway

I knew that at some point I would finally cross paths with the rat. It would be at that moment that I would have to come to terms with my own morality. Could I be so cold, so callous to end this creature's life with one swift blow? In turn, freeing me of the swollen eyes and developing lunacy that had set in since its unwelcome arrival. I am squeamish at times, and was worried about the potential rodent guts that could spill across the hallway with a forceful enough strike. I remained conflicted while the rat chewed on.

At three in the morning my patience had expired. The moral debate had been settled by a surge of anger. I opened the door, no longer slowed by the anchors of petty and childish fears, weapon clasped tight, flicking on the lights to reveal my enemy. He was not on the ground as I expected. Perched on the top of the doorframe, the rat stared back, eyes bulging in its head; heart beat visible and rapid in its tiny body. I met its gaze with a fiery hatred, calling to my roommate for reinforcement. We had it cornered. I stood poised, ready to attack. The rat remained perched, looking on in panic. Thoughts of empathy began to surge, but were quelled by my more immediate rage and desire to finally be rid of the pest. The rat then jumped from its perch.

The first swing was a miss, wild and vengeful, more passion than precision. The rat, darting between our legs, headed for the kitchen. I turned, swinging again with more deliberateness in my strike. This one was a hit. The rat let out a shrill squeak, an unholy wail, as it's small body slammed against the wall, stunning it momentarily. I cocked the stick back for another swing, but the rat recovered and darted towards the kitchen, swerving as it ran, clearly a bit shaken from the initial blow. The barbaric hunt continued from the hall way through the dining room towards the kitchen, my roommate and I chasing after wildly, but the rat was gone already.

The next morning the exterminator was called. The decision was made partially out of necessity and partially out of meekness, as none of my roommates or I thought we could actually kill the rat given the opportunity. They arrived in the afternoon, and after receiving our information surveyed the damage and began setting traps. I was skeptical at first of their process. We had bought traps, setting them baited with peanut butter, but the rat had managed to lick them clean without setting them. The exterminators assured us that this time they would work, leaving us with a two hundred dollar bill as a vote of confidence.

It happened that night. I stirred as the late evening was transitioning into early morning. I felt deeply unsettled knowing that the rat's doom was approaching, the great arrows of death fletched and aimed. The feeling was temporary though, as absolute darkness ran over my eyes and I dove into the vapid pools of the subconscious, no longer fettered about a poor rodent's fate.

The sound was quick and sharp: a sudden snap, a violent death rattle. My pattern awakening was not due to chewing this time, but to the rat's final gasps. Feet scraping at the floor, the rat writhed as the iron bar of the trap crushed the air out of its lungs. Again, my head was jammed between pillows, hidden in horror, hearing the struggle through the walls. This time I had no anger for the rat, only sorrow. I found it tragic that in those final moments with the rat, and throughout the days it had occupied my house, I never had any desire to hear it when I tried to sleep, or for it to even be around. What an unfortunate and terrible existence, I thought, to be deemed unwanted eternally. The rat, which had taken the fall for the flea, to be forever despised, genetically disadvantaged with no redeeming aesthetics or features. In my sadness. I shed a tear for the rat, glad that he would no longer be filling my nights with unwanted racket, but ultimately quite upset and the rat's permanent misfortune.

The rat's frantic fight for life grew less and less. It's feet slowed gradually, and the hallway was suddenly struck with silence. It was over. I didn't go into the hallway like my roommates to inspect the carnage. Instead I went outside, mixing a drink, lighting a cigarette, knowing that the night would again be sleepless.

In the morning the rat's body was not in the trap. It had been collected, placed in a brown paper bag and set upon the doorstep for the exterminator to collect. When I returned from work in the afternoon the bag was gone. The rat had left us, left the house, left the world. And with the casual discarding of a life like yesterday's crumpled news, my life with the rat ended like my life with most things, inconsequentially.

Ageless

She starts to move like she's twenty, fingers in the air, snapping, waist swinging to the lazy one-four-five of the bass. She steps gently, but deliberately. Although she's approaching senior citizenship, approaching slow Sunday drives and restricted diets, she feels like a child moving through all that music, swept up in serenity. Her joints don't sway with the same ease of younger years and she might have put a little weight on her hips, but the woman was compelled upward.

Wrinkles creased his high cheekbones. He looked at her with first time eyes that shone brightly when he smiled at her request to dance. He took her hand, his round the waist and swung through the room with unapologetic youthfulness, silently beaming. The music was irresistible and whispers of pure, ageless love dance between their graying gazes.

Their kids don't call much anymore and the house bellows lonely creaks on windy nights. They are older and sagging. They find it hard to get out of bed on winter mornings, but their affection is timelessness. She gets up early to put on water for his tea in the morning and when his hands aren't seized with arthritis, he sits her down for back rubs at the end of the day. She says he's putting her on and jokes that he'll leave her for a younger woman, but he assures that she's still sexy.

When the youngest daughter asks her about love, she presents the artifacts of romance, testaments to true love. She's proud of her trophy, balding, hiding behind thick glasses. She doesn't even mind his snoring. The most uneducated archeology could dig up and dust off resounding conclusions, bearing witness to a soul mirroring reciprocation in another.

They keep swaying, shaking. The music is contemporary, but the evening feels eternal. The heavenly band, all old boys, creaking in the racket. She keeps up too. Always swinging her body back around on the first count, feet in the right place, eyes still locked on his. Somehow he always forgets what a good dancer she is. But she's always had a way on her feet, back to when a dollar could buy you a bus ticket to Portland, instead of two hours on a parking meter.

In those days, she didn't have to ask him to dance. Her spell was unmistakable, wrapped in a tight dress, pearls and curls and legs that claimed ownership on wandering eyes. She insists that time is cruel when she flips through old photo albums, but he assures that like fine wines or George Clooney, age has only increased her appeal. He jokes that he was lucky enough to know that girl once upon a time, and happened to say enough right and wrong things to grow old with her, and he wouldn't trade that for anything. To watch their children grow and the world change, hand in hand.

She's a bit tipsy by last call and holds onto him real tight as they leave. He searches for keys in his jacket until she pulls him away toward her eyes to tell him he's lovely. They kiss once and then again for good measure, not concerned if anyone is watching them. He takes her hand, guiding her to the passenger side, twirling her round one last time before pulling away. They don't talk on the ride home, radio off, just the passing night and hands clenched above the clutch. The kitchen lights are still on when they pull up. Coats are hung and she puts on tea, while he has a cigarette on the porch. The moon slips in through their bedroom window and they hold each other as they drift off to sleep.

I pay my tab and wonder who would ever dance with me.

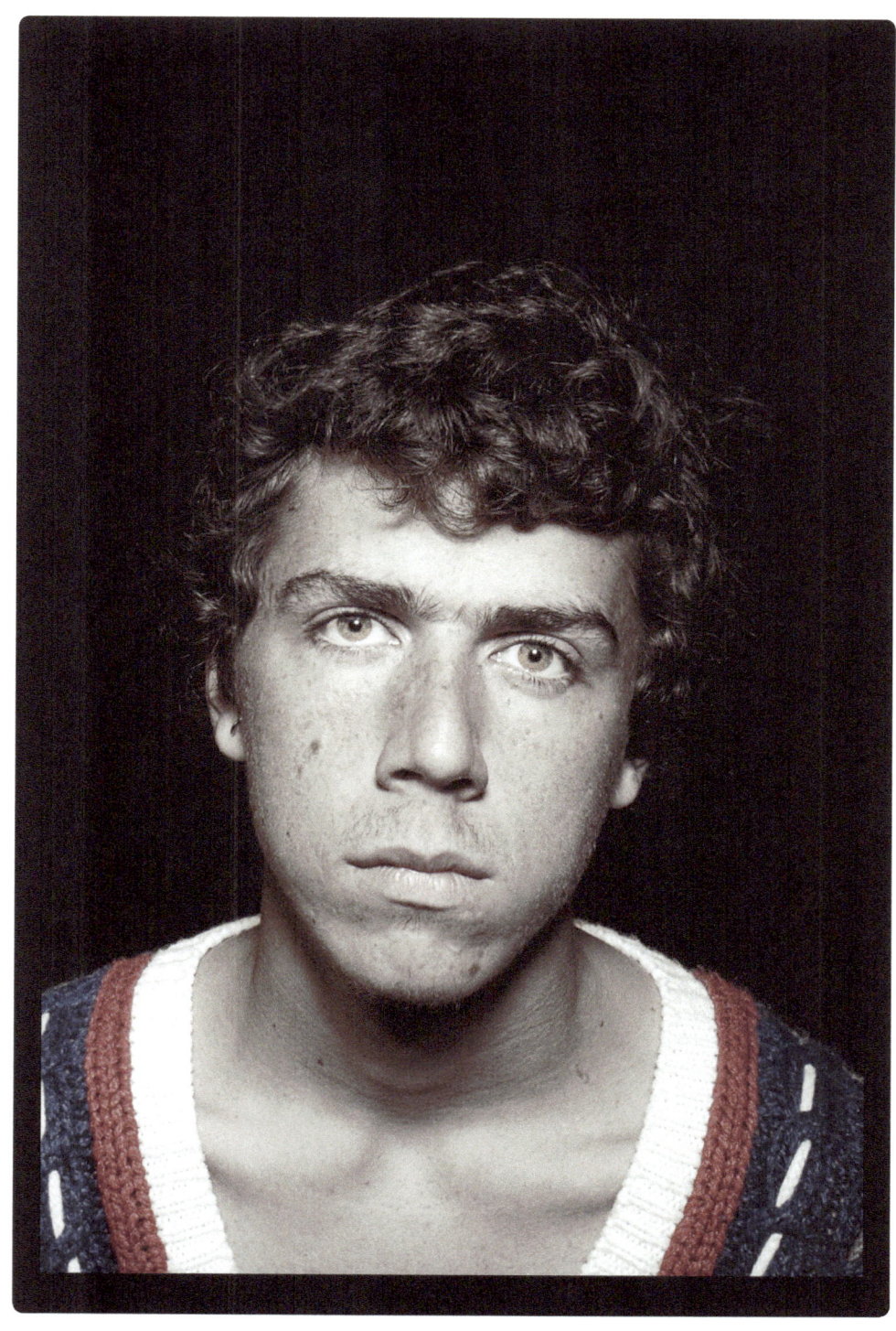

Nihilist Vision

In the stacks, between Dante and Darwin. That's where we would usually meet. In one of the darker corners of the library, tucked away from the crawling public eyes.

She wore satin dresses and her hair down. On the days we would meet, she'd neglect to wear stockings, because I told her that her legs were endless and beautifull.

She was a lot older than me, I didn't care to ask how much older, but she had to be at least thirty. I was nineteen, and knew that what we were doing was taboo and perverse, and that turned me on. It kept me coming back, ducking into the stacks between Dante and Darwin.

Often when we fucked I asked her if we could meet at her place sometime. She told me that she had no interest in seeing me unless I was inside her. I told her to use me. I didn't give a shit about anything, then. I worked a dead end job in a dead end town, living in a dead end apartment with my dead end parents. I told her she could suck me dry of any notions of romantic love, because I was convinced that it didn't exist. There was only want and dirty, animal lust. She pressed me up against the paperbacks and undid my belt.

The town I live in is a cage. Its people fill me with anger, always talking for the sake of talking. Its sidewalks and strip malls make me lonely. The sun that washes over it makes me nauseous, and its nine small streets are an infernal hell.

But I like the library. The quiet calm. The crinkled pages. The smell of books, old and new. People minding their own business, or discussing the gossip floating through the town.It's a sanctuary from the dark of the world. A nest for raw, unshaped ideas to be nourished.

The first time I ever bothered visiting the library was a year and a half ago. That's when I first saw her. Working behind the front desk. Pecking at the computer, helping a small Hispanic child check out books on Star Wars. It was cute. She was patient and sweet. Her hair was up, her face hidden behind thick glasses. She was a spitting archetype of a librarian, just younger. Sexier. There was something crawling to get out from beneath her tight dress and cardigan. And I wanted to set that beast free. Let it loose in the streets, through the stacks, let it devour me whole.

When I approached the desk I was fidgeting with me hair, like I always do. Messing it up to give myself the appearance that I had just gotten out of bed, or that I just didn't give two shits, which I didn't.

"How can I help you?" She smiled.

" What sort of books do you check out when you have a month of house arrest?" I asked casually.

She paused. "A criminal? How dangerous and exciting."

"Hardly. My deadbeat friends are the real crooks. Turns out driving your thieving buddies away from a crime scene is somewhat legally obtuse," I laughed.

"You're only as good as the company you keep, you know," She said, returning to the computer, "but I emphasize with your situation. I've had my own legal mishaps," She trailed off, "Anyway, I don't know what your reading habits are but I would imagine that you're going to need a lot of books to occupy a whole month. Go find these," She said handing me a piece of paper covered in scribbled call numbers.

I returned to the desk, arms full of titles that didn't mean anything to me then, but would become my closest friends during my winter sentence.

"You seem like a guy who would like Kerouac," she told me as she pointed to the book on top of the stack of paperbacks. "Restless, full of youth and life. I bet you smoke weed too. Turn on some jazz, like NPR or something, roll a joint and read this," She said, pointing to a book called, 'The Dharma Bums.' "I like to read Kerouac aloud. You can hear all the little nuances of his speech patterns, gives you a real sense of his brilliance as a writer. Make sure to read 'Tropic of Cancer,' too." Pointing to another, "It's so sexy, and dirty. Henry Miller just runs around Paris, drinking. writing, and sleeping with anything with a pulse. And he writes like a man. I hate those mushy, overly sensitive male writers. Miller writes like he could be trying to fuck you with his pen."

"Sure," I shrugged, collecting the books, amused by her honesty, and profoundly curious about this strange woman.

"I'll see you in a month," she laughed. "Let me know if you like those." I nodded, exchanging gazes with her. I told her that I didn't know librarians were so cool. She laughed and told me I was being too sweet, as she was definitively 'uncool'. Arms heavy with books, I turned from the counter, her smile heavy in my head.

I might have killed myself if it weren't for those books. I didn't read a single book in high school, but as soon as I jumped into those worn pages, I found an escape from the morbid and stale reality that surrounded me. My house was a prison, a fortress. I wore an ankle bracelet that tracked my movements, keeping me shackled within those four maddening walls.Nothing changed. The sky was gray, always. My parents left in the morning. They came home at night. I fed my cat twice. I had a bowl of cereal and watched VH1 marathons in the morning. I took online classes in the afternoon, and when I didn't have an assignment I would masturbate, or do crosswords, or whatever the fuck I could find to pass the time. In the evening we would eat dinner, and it would be the same thing day after day after day. Purgatory.

With the coming of night, when darkness settled outside my window and I could no longer see the world passing me by, the world that I was no longer a part of, I would succumb to complete escapism and fall through the open doorways of those books. When I finished one I jumped to the next, each one more brilliant than the last. Each one detailing lives defined by freedom, and each one reminding me of her.

And as the spring crawled over the grey town, I emerged from my solitude. No longer a prisoner, ankle no longer anchored by its burdensome bracelet. Free. Though the notion of freedom was much more thrilling than the actual reality. The town was still the same stale gray, same stale people walking the streets. I felt inspired though, brain now full of brilliant stories, wild notions, no longer weighed down by my insatiable nihilism. I walked to the library to turn in all my books in person. I wanted to see if she was working.

To my great pleasure, she was there, right where I'd left her. Sitting behind the desk. Pecking at the computer. She saw me and smiled. I had stopped caring much about my appearance and had let my hair long and my facial hair grow scraggly.

"Welcome back to real life," she smiled. "You look older, it suits you." I had stopped caring much about my appearance and had let my hair grow long and my facial hair scraggly.

"You look beautiful," I told her.

"My. That's awfully sweet. And bold," She laughed nervously.

"The view in apartment 122 isn't known for its aesthetics. Now that I'm out everything in this town has a bit of a brighter sheen to it, a bit more life," I laughed staring at her. She was blushing. "Thank you."

"For what?" She asked, shifting her gaze away from her computer.

"For giving me a reason to not put a bullet in my head," I said plainly. "Those books saved my life. You must be a damn good librarian, because they were exactly what I needed."

"Oh no. Those are just the books I read when I was your age. I suppose I felt the same way about them then too," she laughed.

"Can you help me find more?" I asked.

"Come with me," She motioned toward the stacks. She tugged at my shirt, hand running over my chest – just lightly enough to seem accidental, but her touch lingered, revealing ulterior purpose.

I followed closely behind her. I was electrified by our brief physical contact. I could sense some dynamic connection, a powerful magnetism stirring between us. Watching her long legs swing back and forth. She stopped and turned around and I immediately shook my head upward, so she wouldn't think I was staring at her ass, which I was.I walked in through the aisle of books, expecting her to walk away, but she stayed and watched me look through the vast sea of books.

"I think I've got in from here," I told her.

"Oh, you don't like my company?" She said, stepping closer.

"No by all means. I'll get lost in here," I laughed. "Besides," turning to face her, "a girl like you couldn't be bad company if you tried."

" A girl like me?" she asked in a bedroom whisper. She was very close now. Standing right in front of me. I could smell her perfume. See her great big green eyes behind her thick black glasses.

"You seem like a guy who needs all the help he can get," She said. "I thought about you a lot this winter. Wondering if you'd come in again. Those books were overdue, you know. And we just can't have that. There are consequences for that sort of behavior" Her breath was hot on my neck. Her body was now pressed against my chest. She took her hair down. It was gorgeous, long and flowing.

"It must've been lonely being stuck in your house for that long. No one to take good care of you. I bet you thought about me. I could tell when you came up to talk to me that you wanted to fuck me," She whispered in my ear in between kissing my neck. I coughed. I was overwhelmed. I was turned on. I was in over my head.

"I see your mom come in here from time to time. I bet she wouldn't like me too much," She said as she stuck her hands down my pants.

She pushed me further back into the stacks, up against the shelves. She und c my belt. She unzipped my jeans, pulling them down to mid-thigh with the deliberateness of an expert. She closed her eyes and I looked down the row of books to my left, recoiling in ecstasy. Paradiso.

Before I walked out of the library she told me to meet her there the same time next week. I drove home slowly. I felt a vivid current coursing through me. Puffing on cigarette, trying to make sense of exactly what had just transpired.

I showed up the next week, and the week after that. Again and again. Each time she wanted more. She asked me to start meeting her twice a week. My mom commented, "Boy, you sure like going to the library. It's good that you're so getting so into reading."

"Yeah. I can't keep away from those books," I laughed.

We were never caught. The time I would meet her was close to the time they closed, and there was another person working the desk, so she could steal away with me. Though, with women, and moreover with the library, there are always complications.

"How long are we going to keep this up?" I asked her, zipping up my pants.

"Am I boring you?" She asked.

"No. No. It's just, is this all this will ever be? Are fucking other guys, and just counting on me to show up and satisfy you on the side?"

"Oh honey, grow up," She said, condescendingly. "I'm never going to date you. This is not some bizarre love story. This is purely physical. And if you have a problem with that, you don't have to meet me here ever again."

"No, I mean I don't have a problem with it. It's just a bit crazy for me. My parents ask me if I'm seeing someone all the time. 'What's a handsome young guy like you doing single?' they ask. And I just smile and tell them that I'm not worried about it right now."

"It's sounds like you're worried about it," she said coldly.

"Look," I was getting frustrated. "Don't be a bitch."

"I thought you could be a man about our arrangement," she said, buttoning her blouse. "Obviously I was wrong."

"I could get you fired, you know. One word, and you'd be done here."

"You wouldn't dare, you little brat," she spat.

"Fine. You're right. I wouldn't, but I'm leaving. Let go off my shirt please. If you see me here again, please let me go about my business. I'm not gonna go and run my mouth around town, or tell my parents and friends. If anyone found out, it would compromise both us."

"Alright. Get out of here then," she scoffed.

And as easily as I had walked into her life, I walked out. Through the doors, out into the streets. Away from the books I loved, and back into my nihilistic visions of what I called real life. I had my mom pick my books up from then on. Sometimes I would pass her, driving down the road. We would both look straight ahead, fully aware of one another's presence, but either too embarrassed or bitter to smile back.

Sometimes these things are riddled with impermanence. The same way we can fall into a story, we can slip into someone else's life, if only for a moment, eventually to return them to the shelves of the world, and sneak out the back door. Try as we might, there are things that will never change in this world. We have no control of the attractions that find us. We must take each moment in stride and soak it all in for what it's worth. We can only celebrate the magnificence of a moment as it occurs, and once it's gone, it is gone. There is no point longing after it, even if it looks good in a mini-skirt. We might be able to change the people that we are, but we will never be able to change the things of such immensity, like the nature of the human heart, the ocean, or the stars.

Savannas

The young boy would spend hot days like this on his back. Eyes skyward, he looked out at the vast clouds forming over the Mediterranean from his shaded roof.

Other boys his age were down by the water, or playing soccer in the neighboring fields, kicking up dust, laughing. They didn't care much for him. There weren't any discernibly negative qualities to the boy, but the others in the town seemed to think he was strange. "Too quiet," they would agree.

The boy's family had moved north to Tangier only several months before. His mother and father, ever-aging grandfather, two brothers and a sister all lived under the same roof. His siblings attended school, but his parents decided that he was not old enough. In actuality, they still couldn't afford him proper dress to attend the formal elementary. "There is nothing that you cannot learn from your elders and through hard work that you can learn in some fancy school, Son," his father affirmed.

The boy disagreed though, not to his father's face, as he would surely strike him. But as he gazed up at the thick, ballooned clouds, questions would spring to his mind like grasshoppers up from the hot streets. "Why are the clouds always different?' He would ask his father as they walked towards the market.

"Because God decided them to be that way," his father explained, a resolute and uncurious man.

"Where do clouds go? Where do they come from?" To his mother in the kitchen.

"It doesn't matter, now help your sister prepare supper," she scolded, handing him a plate of whole carrots and onions.

With each day, more questions would flood the boy's young mind. When he stared up at the looming clouds, he would envision them as great fluffy animals. Some of them he knew from books and memory, others from his grandfather's stories, though he could only guess what the great and horrible 'crocodile' actually looked like, as his image of it was only a second-hand description.

At dinner the boy would ask, "When will I be able to attend school like my brothers and the other boys in the town?"

"When you are older, my son," his mother would say between bites of their dinner of fish and vegetables.

"But Mother, that is the same thing you said the last time I asked." Silence settled around the table as the family stirred at their plates unresponsively. "Aren't I growing older everyday? I am almost one month older from the day I last asked for permission to attend school. What will happen when I can't get older, how will I be able to go to school then?"

"It won't matter then, will it?" The grandfather wheezed.

"But what if my head gets too full of questions? What if there is no room for answers, and I'll never be able to know where the clouds hide on clear days?"

"Enough," the father said firmly. "You will attend school when we say so."

"Oh let the poor boy go," the grandfather said, lighting a cigarette.

"That is not for you to decide, Yousef," the boy's mother said, collecting plates from the table.

"He needs to be around children his age. He needs to be playing, and laughing, and getting into the trouble that young boys are so keen at finding," as he spoke ash fluttered down from the table, catching the boys attention.

"I need him to help me at the market. And besides, he does not have the proper clothes; I cannot afford them without his help. I will not have my son showing up in rags," the father said.

"Let him! And let them laugh if they will! They'll see, see how smart little Amal is." He turned to the boy still distracted by the falling ash. "Remember, boy. You are never the clothes on your back, but the heart in your chest. Do you understand?" The boy nodded and cleared their plates.

The father leaned across the table while the boy washed up after supper with his brothers and sister. "He will not go. I need his help now, school will be there for him when we've passed through this hard season."

"Do you sense that it is a warm year? The fisherman will catch, the fish will fly from your stand. You are always so wracked with worry, Son. Do you want that for Amal? Don't you want him to have a childhood as you did?"

"He will help me till I am satisfied, and I will not have another word on the matter,' he said, storming from the kitchen.

The grandfather called after, "You don't want him to resent you!" Sitting in the stale air of the kitchen, he lit another cigarette, took a long drag, put it out and went upstairs to bed.

The young boy woke up early yet again, as it was too hot to sleep. He pulled on the same shirt he wore yesterday, stinking of sweat from hauling ice from the docks the previous morning. He sighed in frustration, mad at himself that he hadn't washed his clothes the night before. He sauntered up the stairs by his bedroom door, through another door and up the last steps to the roof.

The sun was already blazing unmercifully, cooking the drunks next door out from their dark rooms, squinting in the brightness. The boy's grandfather was stretched out in the old chair made of reeds, hidden from the harsh heat, feet resting on the raised wall of the roof. He was reading the worn book of poetry that he carried with him often. The book had always fascinated the boy. It was old and worn, leather-bound, dull and tattered as the hands that held it. The pages were all handwritten, some with stains, ink, among other things. He jolted from the book when the boy stirring nearby surprised him.

"Oh! Mercy, Amal, you gave me an awful fright. What are you doing up this early?"

"It's too hot to sleep, and father will be up soon, surely with chores for me before we go to the market."

"It is much too hot," he agreed.

"Grandfather, why don't you read the holy texts like my father?" The boy asked, curiously.

He paused, marking his place in the old book and setting it on the ground, "You may not know this now, but your father, my son, he is a worried man. He is an uncertain man, who does not believe that he can even count on the stars to shine on clear nights. But he is dutiful. Dutiful to this family. Dutiful to our God. He believes that his faith is the only thing that he can always count on. He believes that even through the struggles he faces everyday, if he cannot achieve the life he feels he rightfully deserve, his devotion to God will reward him in death."

"But I am much too old to worry about the life that surrounds me. I am graying, and have numbered days. Wherever I am destined to go has long been decided. I have committed wrongs in my long life, but have also strived for good, and whatever may happen to me I will accept with resolution. So I find faith in the past that has brought me to this very moment." He grabbed the book from the ground. "These are my grandfather's writings – poems and scribbled verses, musings about life and death, love and loss. He wrote many things when he was young, and told me many stories of the world before I was born, as I like to tell you on the cool evenings after dinner. They are as comforting as food in my stomach or the clothes on my back, because they remind me that our experience as humans and on this earth remains true through the years for all mankind. The challenges we face, and the goodness we revel."

"But Grandfather, aren't you scared to die? Father says that without faith there will be no one to guide us to the afterlife."

"I am as scared to die as any man. But we must remember that death is the greatest uncertainty of life, and can be perceived as a horrifying and abrupt extinguishing of a candle, or as the footsteps towards the next most beautiful adventure beyond this realm. Look here, Amal." He said, flipping through the book.

The boy peered over his Grandfather's shoulder at the worn pages, and read, "Today I wept for what feels the first time. Mother has passed on, and her spirit rises out of her now quiet body into the universe amongst the stars. Today I feel no fear. Death's touch is swift and unapologetic, but memory survives our time on earth, and we hold it close for answers and comfort. We must not perceive death in anguish, but as the long journey home – April 5."

"That's very beautiful, Grandfather. Your Grandfather was a very wise man."

"He was. I loved him greatly," He smiled, and then pulled the young boy close, hugging him. "And I love you very much as well, Amal. Now run along to help your father."

The boy turned to the stairs. "Amal," He called after him.

The boy came back, "Yes?"

"Take these," he said, handing him a small pouch of coins from his chest pocket.

"Grandfather–"

"Take them. I have no use for money to spend. You will go to the tailors near the port. Ask them for Salima. She is an old friend. She will fit you with clothes suitable to attend the elementary. Do this now as she will be busy through out the day, I will tell your father that I sent you for cigarettes."

The boy looked at the money weighing down his hand, and then again to his grandfather. "This is too kind, too much entirely."

"This is what's right, Amal. You are too smart of a boy to be slaving at the markets with your father. You should be learning language and arithmetic, and of course about your beloved clouds," he said, ruffling the boy's hair.

"I am so grateful, Grandfather. I will make you proud," and with a word he was gone.

The boy went to Salima's, a tiny boutique near the water. The door and windows were all propped open to keep cool air coming in from the ocean. Inside the elderly woman worked tirelessly, with threads and needles in hand, the younger women bringing fabric, cutting loose thread, studying the older ones' hands as they weaved through the material. The boy approached one of the women.

"Hello, my name is Amal. am the grandson of Yousef. Can you help me find Salima?"

"Heavens! Little Amal, what a treat to see you again," the woman bent down to his eye level, and the boy assumed she must be Salima. "The last time I laid eyes on you were no bigger than an eggplant. How you've grown," she pinched his cheek. "What can I do for you?"

"I need clothes for school. Trousers and a collared shirt, can you make those?"

"Better than anyone in this town. Sit down here so I can take some of your measurements."

Salima sat him down and wrapped a measuring tape around his chest and arms and neck, along his arms and around his wrists. Waist to armpit and shoulder to shoulder. She wrote everything down on a small piece of paper on the neighboring desk. She then had him sit up, and took the measurements for his legs, all with the same precision she applied to his upper body. He watched her hands, old and leathery like his grandfather's that moved with such deliberateness. They ran along his legs, pulling at the tape, holding it taught with one hand, and scribbling notes with the other. It took all of a minute before Salima collected her things and told the boy she was done.

The boy handed her the small pouch of coins, "Come back at sundown today, the clothes will be ready then." He ran all the way home, excitement surging through him. His grandfather was waiting at the front door of their house. "Did you find her?"

"I did Grandfather, I did. She's making them right now!" The boy gasped.

"Wonderful, well I will pick them up for you, as to not distract you from helping your father at the market, and tomorrow we will go to the elementary to register you for the upcoming term."

"Oh what a wonderful day! Thank you a thousand times, Grandfather!" He hugged him and ran inside. His mother had mint tea, with bread, jams and olives waiting at the table. The boy, invigorated with the excitement of the morning feasted wildly.

"What an appetite you have this morning, Amal," his mother commented.

"Today is wonderful, Mother. I must have the proper strength to meet it," he spoke between big bites and gulps.

His father came in the room, fresh from the bath, grabbing a piece of bread with jam, "Are you ready son?" He asked moving towards the door.

"Coming father," said the boy, collecting his things for the day.

Down at the market, the sun worked tirelessly to pierce through the shade of the tents propped up to protect the vendors' goods. The boy would travel to the port nearby, pushing his father's cart to collect ice to keep the fish cold. The first catch of the morning was delivered to the stand, shortly after they had arrived to set up. By the afternoon more fish would come in, unless it was a slow day, and they would pack up early, freezing the fish that were not sold, taking the rest of the morning's catch home for supper.

"Alas, Son, today is as slow as the drip of molasses," his father said after many had browsed through the market, moving the now frozen fish towards the idle cart. "Go home now boy, find freedom in the long day."

The boy cast the iced, weighted fish in his hands towards the stationary cart, and smiled, "Surely, Father. I will see you at supper time."

Each footstep was laced with excitement. Not directed towards the water as usual when the day was short, but quickly towards home to hear from his grandfather. Back up the cobbled alley, teeming with desire.

He went through the door, oblivious to his sister already with a knife to a mackerel's head, preparing the fish for supper. His grandfather was as he left him, feet along the raised roof, cigarette loose from his mouth, worn book nearby, "Grandfather, grandfather, I am done for the day. Have you retrieved my clothes?" he gasped, exasperated.

"Amal, my boy, please catch you breath," he demanded, as he saw the boy, clutching his knees reaching for air. Then holding up a crumpled paper sack he smiled, "They are right here."

The boy peered in the bag to see a neatly folded pair of trousers and a fine collard shirt inside. A smile sprang to his face. Throwing his arms around his grandfather he exclaimed, "This is the absolute greatest! What a kind, old soul you have! I love you, grandfather."

"A boy with a brain like you must be given the chance to learn as soon as his mind grows restless, rather than squandering his gifts of curiosity and intelligence toiling in the markets, slinging fish."

"This day only continues to get better. The only thing I could want more is a story from my generous and dear grandfather."

"I don't know, Amal. Don't you want to play with the other boys at the seaside?"

"No. They are not nearly as interesting or kind as you. Please, grandfather, just one story, before supper, before father comes home and demands I help him prepare for tomorrow."

He lit another cigarette, "Do you remember the life we lead before moving north?" He asked.

"No," the boy shook his head. "I was only a baby."

"Of course." He said, taking a long drag, shifting his chair towards the ocean and setting sun, "Well, before you were born, your grandmother and I lived happily together."

"I know so little about my grandmother. What was she like?"

"She was beautiful and fair. Kind and thoughtful, like your mother. I miss her more with each day I grow older, Amal."

"One day you will meet in the next life, then?" He asked.

"We will, and I look forward to that day," He smiled. "But. many years ago, before you walked this earth, and before even your father was born I was a strong, broad-shouldered man. I was powerful and brave, and looked after my wife, your grandmother as we first began to start a family. "

"When the sun was first rising, she would walk a great distance to collect water for the day, carrying cumbersome jugs to and fro. It was the only means to keep our thirsts quenched, our bodies clean, and our stomach's full. It was harsh and severe, each day providing difficult challenges, but we were young and able bodied, motivated to keep each other healthy and well," He paused, another deep inhale of his cigarette, examining his aged body. "It startles me now, to think of myself then. Age is a cruel mistress, Amal. As the years continue to pass, we are endowed the pleasures of learning through the same eyes we are born with, constantly growing internally and through the sensation and experiences that surround us. But to exist fully and truly, with wonder and a full heart. the body we reside in burdens an immense toll. You have a long full life ahead of you, Amal. Find yourself in the moment of everyday,' He stopped, and after a grip of silence, the boy still listening intently, watching the smoke drift up from his grandfather's cigarette towards the clear sky. Suddenly he began to laugh, "Look at me, I was in the middle of a story, rambling off like an old man. I'm sorry Amal, let me continue."

"On one particular morning, your grandmother had left to fetch water. The night before was marked with the heaviest rain yet of the season, the ground still loose and muddy from the storm, the path towards the drinkable pools of water, churned up from other women. As she returned, her body tired from the long day of tilling and planting the day before, she lost grasp of the heavy jug – made of a thin layer of clay, big enough to hold at least four large pots of water. She slipped on the worn trail, and the jug crashed upon her angle, severely breaking it."

"I had been working the crops, and found it strange that my wife had not returned fairly quickly, as usual, but was so immersed in my work that my concern was brief, as I returned to the labor at hand. Another woman, a close friend of your grandmother's, happened to walking a long the trail much later than usual, as she had had a long night before, helping her niece who delivered a child that evening. She found your grandmother alone, near the path, crying in agony, exhausted from the heat. She had managed to crawl beneath the shade of a tree, but was suffering a great deal. The woman who found her brought her water from the neighboring pools, and then hurried back to the village to find me."

"When the news was broke, I was off as fast as the lighting that showered the sky the night before. I know it may seem hard to imagine your grandfather moving with the grace of a gazelle,"– The boy tried to recall an image of the gazelle from another of his grandfather's stories, but could not – "but as I said, I was young and virile in those days." He put out his cigarette and turned to the boy.

"I raced down the muddy path, careless of slipping. The daylight was shorter in that time of year, so I knew I had to travel quickly. You see, it as at nightfall when the Lions begin to hunt, and it is near water that they are known find prey. When I found my wife she was praying through tears. I hugged her at first sight, cursing her misfortune. I carefully hoisted her into my arms, as she was of delicate frame, and started back down the trail. I sang to her, songs of my childhood, to distract from the pain of her ankle, which by then had swollen to the size of a melon. "

"About a mile outside of the village, dusk had begun to settle. Calls of birds signal the folding of the final light, and the coming of complete darkness. The savanna stirred with settling and awakening life. Carrying my wife I grew nervous of surrounding danger."

"Were you scared, Grandfather?" The boy asked.

"Yes, Amal. I was very scared for both of our lives. I had heard many stories of unfortunate souls crossing paths of a hungry lion at night, some who lived to bring their tale to my ears, others, whose tales could only be told by the families that survived them."

"But the lions cannot always be mean, like the angry crocodile? Can they?"

"No. The Lion is a proud creature. It is king of its domain, and rules with clenching jaws and powerful roar. It is intelligent and graceful, so strong and fearless. The lion has no predator. Before man so callously harnessed the power of the spark, to propel lead with the intention of death, he would not dare cross the lion. But I will tell you this, boy: A hungry predator is a hungry predator, and nothing is more dangerous than a desperate animal that thirsts for blood."

He continued, "A rustling in the bushes was only the first troubling sign. Then two eyes, yellow, glowing harvest moons, darting, blinking with each step closer.It was female, skinny and snarling. Her mouth was agape, looking for a morsel, probably for cubs, which would have been all the worse. Starving cubs only furthers a mother's predatory desperation. I stood absolutely still, clutching your grandmother, arrested in terror. The lioness was so close I could smell hot breath off of her. The breath has a haunting urgency when laced with hunger. I wanted so badly to run, but it would be foolish, as the lion would chase after, costing both our lives. I was steadfast, trying to show my courage for my wife's sake. Her head was buried in my chest, and as she turned to face the approaching animal, she let out a whimper. Body seizing up, I lurched back. The lioness did not pounce, but slinked backwards as well. Suddenly, the crack of a branch in the distance rang out, like an angel's cry." – He smacked the table, startling the boy. "Attention drawn elsewhere, the lioness turned from the path, off into the brush, and then gone. My knees shook violently, arms barely able to carry my wife. As soon as I felt it was safe I kicked from the path, running as hard and as fast as I could. I could tell she was in pain, wincing as I hurried through the darkness, but she understood my desire to make it home as fast as possible. I ran far faster than my legs had ever carried me, ran until I could see the fires from the village. I didn't stop until I was out the door of our small house. Laying your grandmother down, I breathed a great sigh of relief. I kissed her a thousand times, thankful that nothing terrible had happen. Of course once my heart had calmed in my chest, I was reminded that my wife's foot was still injured. Retrieving wood to make a brace, and cloth to wrap it, I tended to her malady with care and precision. Though she howled, she showed great strength. The night was not restful, but ever dutiful to my wife, we arrived at the city two days later for proper treatment."

A large pile of ash had collected at their feet from the grandfather's cigarettes. The two of them sat in silence for a great time. Separately, they boy and his grandfather struggled to fully envision the story, as it was a life unknown to the boy, and through the passing of many years, equally so to the grandfather. Finally the boy spoke, "That was a wonderful story, Grandfather. I have never heard you talk of your past or of Grandmother with such passion."

"That is because they are two things that I can no longer have, Amal."

The two sat for a moment longer, and then the boy spoke. "It is beginning to cool off, don't you think?" The sun, now nearly entirely set off to the east. The boy and his grandfather caught the smells of sizzling fish coming from the kitchen below them and with hungry eyes agreed to go downstairs to join the rest of the family. The boy's mother had set the table and his brothers were in the den studying.

"Where have you been all day, Amal?" His mother asked.

"Father sent me home early, so I have been listening to Grandfather's stories this afternoon."

"That sounds lovely, Son," who had gone to the sink to wash his hands and face. She turned to his grandfather, "More tales of the Savanna? All your wild stories are no good for the boy."

"Oh, what harm can they do? If he does nothing but think of chores and the market, his mind will grow as stale as old bread. He needs something that allows his mind to wander and imagine a life more fantastic than his own."

"Fine," she agreed stubbornly, returning to the stove.

Still holding the brown bag of clothes, the grandfather attempted to sneak off to his room to keep it safe from the boy's parents. "What's that you've got there?" The boy's mother asked.

"Oh, it's nothing. If you must know, stationary to write to my remaining relatives," He said, hiding it behind his back.

"What farce!" She cried. "Give it here. You've no one to write to." She lunged for the back, quicker than the grandfather's slow hands, prying it from his grasp. Peaking in, the color drained from her pointed face. "This is unacceptable, Yousef! The nerve. The audacity! To go behind the back of my husband, the boy's father! And with what money! Have you secretly been hoarding a fortune while your own son slaves away selling stinking fish at the market?" She was livid. The boy stood frozen in the doorway to the kitchen seeing the looks of guilt and anger and his grandfather and mother's faces. She turned to him, pointing to his room, "Now, before I completely loose my temper. No supper. And I would advise you to consider that fair, because you may not be treated so kindly when your father gets news of this blatant disrespect."

"Please, this was my doing," his grandfather father pleaded.

"I will not hear another word from you, Yousef. And you can find yourself food to fill your fat belly. Clearly you have the money to do so," She scorned, eyes like daggers.

Before the boy could hear another word, his grandfather motioned for him to go to his room. Upstairs, he could hear screaming. Then two voices became three. His father was home. Then footsteps up the stairs, towards his room, then the opening of his door.

The boy had never been so scared. The lion was hungry, staring through him with lowered eyes, staring holes through his tiny body. His father entered the room with freight train force, grabbing the boy by the shirt. He slapped him across the face. Then another. Open hands turned to closed fists. The boy could not feel his face. Between the blurs of swinging hands, blood running from his nose, he felt as though he could see the sky through the roof of his bedroom. Blue and endless, dotted with towering clouds, some shaped as animals, the angry crocodile, the unfortunate mackerel, the proud lion, all beckoning him to join them far away the horror unfolding in the tiny bedroom.

The boy's father stopped, face twisted up in fury. He could only look upon the boy, breath coursing through his body. The boy lay back on the bed using his shirt to wipe the blood from his face. The father took one last look at him. a look on his face indicating a search for words, something to say to justify the punishment, but nothing came and he stormed downstairs.

They boy lay back in his bed for an unknowable time. He could still hear raised voices from downstairs.

"How dare you! How dare you disrespect my authority in my own home, you miserable parasite, feeding off of this family's hard work," his father bellowed.

Then came his grandfather's voice, delivered with a power the boy had never heard on his frail breath. "Less you forget, son, that I am the one who raised you. Without help a mother to nurture you, to care for you, to change you, to hold your hand when you were scared of storms at sea. That I had to give you enough love so you could know the spoil and wonder of two parents' hearts, instead of one, feeble and lonely. That I am the one who brought you to this city so you could realize your potential, fed you, clothed you, kept a warm roof over your head during the winter seasons. You have squandered what I tried to give you, chasing foolish dreams instead of filling your mind with useful knowledge, conditioning your hands to build and create instead of strike your own child."

"He is not your child, Yousef."

A smack rang out in the kitchen. "You will address me as father, son, and you will never forget that fact."

There was a chilling quiet through the kitchen. Then the boy's father spoke, "You may have once been a father to me, but you are nothing more than a burden. A delusional, old, lonely man."

His grandfather's voice cracked as he spoke between gasps, "I will not have this. I cannot take what has become of you, what you are doing to this family."

Heavy footsteps trailed up the stairs. The boy sat up from his bed. He heard the steps loose rhythm, stuttering over the stairs. His grandfather stumbled through the hall by the boy's room towards the roof, breathing heavily, clutching at his heart. The boy, unsure of what was going, jumped from his bed. He followed up to the roof gasping at the top stair.

The boy's grandfather had collapsed on the roof, holding his chest. "Grandfather!" The boy screamed. "Grandfather, please be ok!" Tears were running down the boy's face, mixing with the blood drying around his nose and upper lip. His grandfather was breathing hard, cringing has he clutc hed as his heart. "Don't leave me, Grandfather. You can't! You can't!"

The boy screamed for his mother and father. He wailed in agony, his heart so heavy in his throat he felt like he could has vomited all his organs out upon the rooftop. His grandfather was dying. He knew it. Sweat poured down his brow. and his body clenched tight in violent fits.

"Grandfather," He wept. "There is no one more important to me on this planet, and I cannot loose you. I love you, Grandfather."

His grandfather took a long, forced breath, and fought to roll his head towards the boy and jar his eyes open. "Amal," he said weakly. "My sweet, brilliant boy. I am sorry. I am so sorry to leave you like this. I am old and frail though, and my heart cannot suffer any more in this life. I know this seems selfish, but you will understand one day." He was struck by a fit of coughs. Turning to the boy, again. "Take this," handing him the worn book from his pocket. "I will not be able to tell you any more stories, my boy, but when you miss me, you can find me written all over these old pages.' He continued to struggle for breath.

'Are you scared to die Grandfather?" The boy asked between sobs, clutching the book to his heart.

"No, Amal. My life has been long, and I have given and received love from many, and what man could ask for anything else." His eyes grew wider, "I can hear the lions coming though, Amal. They are so close."

"I am so afraid for you, Grandfather."

"Do not be. Do not live your life as a man afraid to challenge the world. because he is likely to fail, like your father. I love you with all my heart, Amal. You will be a fine man." Raising his arms he ran his hands through the boy's hair. "My sails are set," his breath growing echo, distant, faint as a feather's touch. "I am going home."

Mon Amore

Olympia, you are two glitter pills washed down with cold whisky. A revolving circus of scenes and fiends and codeine dreams. And I'm still always wondering what to do with you at the end of every cigarette.

When we sit down, face to face, I can sense that you must be looking into the eyes of madness and depravity. Though, I'm always impressed at how you've made my self-destruction poetic. Olympia, you've turned us all into weekend warriors, running for the last drunk bus, vegan dogs with cream cheese from Jakes in our guts. But don't worry, my love, there's always another party.

I'm always sure of where I am when I catch the sweet smells of sweat stained afterglow, ethnic spices, black coffee and American Spirits. You've got all that noise splitting out your sides too. Always whispering in the cracks and crevices along 4th. Wailing black banshee death to the writhing hipster concert crowds. Fizzling and snapping like a tall bottle of O.E.

Everyone assures me that it's the water here. Constantly seeping it's way into every nook and cranny of my life. The rain is the only thing I've ever been able to count on in this city. It's as if there is a constant leak in the sky converging overhead. And like the water that spills from the artisan well, day after day, rain runs down the streets, demanding boots and warm jackets.

But Olympia, beneath your concrete carapace and oddities, there is a sleeping smile. There is a warmth that I cannot deny. I have seen you bathed in sun with the sweet smells of spring blooming. I've endured long nights of blurry wonder, singing and dancing out in your streets. I've felt chameleon change burrow under my skin and grab hold of my head, heart and wardrobe. And above all, I've found solace in the brilliant and beautiful minds living in your arms.

There are sometimes when I've reached my fill of you, Olympia. When I find myself squirming in apathy, on the precipice of insanity and the only solution is instantaneous escape, you drive me away. You send me to foreign lands, chaotic streets of Beijing, sprawling cloud canopy of Monte Verde. And once I'm bulging and swollen with new experiences and ideas, I breathe a great sigh of relief, because you are still there waiting for my return, arms open, halo of fog above your head.

Here, at the bottom of the sound, ghosts of reason and normalcy come to rest. Days slip away under the blanket of long winters, an eternal dark. But with soaked shoes we walk onward together, Olympia. Even when you give me your worst, the day breaks and you hand me gems and make me feel like a genius. I'm sorry that I talk badly about you Olympia, because I don't mean it. This is home for now, and Olympia, my heart is yours.

Exoskeletal

Out west in junk-sick nowhere, a hot blip on a sprawling map of insignificance. Wheels heavy to the road, lips loose on the end of a bitter cigarette, eyes sore with the bends, caught imagining too long the depths of her thighs. Blurts of mummified words, castrated consciousness. An entire generation of ideas lined up like pigs for slaughter. A whole godforsaken voyage strangled with stifled conversation and radio mush.

My hands were itching for something, tapping on the steering wheel, restless indecision bouncing through the car. I pulled into a diner, because the atmosphere was too toxic to swallow.

My box of books sat in the back. Crammed full of soft words. Books I'd open up, and every sound I'd ever heard jumped out. Crawling all over me like hungry insects, kissing my eyes. A catalyst for frothy ideas, revelations, pluming out in spires over the long sky. Those I still liked. Two post cards on the dash had the original address crossed out, and she had started painting over the original photos. Those too. I got out, looking back at all the useless shit our lives had amounted to in the past three years. A material sarcophagus that buried us in a landslide of our own greed. The Capitalist condition, I suppose. She fixed her hair in the rear view mirror.

"I'm not hungry." She told me.

I didn't care much. Out here in ghostly nowhere, patience is thin and scarce.I needed stillness and coffee and a minute to think about something more than passing scenery and concrete.

By the time she joined me in the diner, I was sipping my coffee. The first real relief I'd felt in days. A sweet rose in this recent garden of thorns. We sat staring at the menu, listening to the diner creak in skeletal groans. A dumpy old so and so, took our orders and made small talk. She spoke, while I stared out the window into the darkening abyss of land outside.

"We're headed north. Moving up to Chicago." She told her.

"Oh you'll like it there. Cold winters though. Hope you brought your jackets." She warned us, as if we were somehow unaware of the vast chill sweeping over Illinois from the great lakes.

The women retreated to the kitchen, sensing we didn't have much to say.

"Would it kill you to be polite?" She asked me while I vacantly fidgeted with the silverware on the table.

"I don't have anything to say to her. I don't owe her any conversation." I said, still staring downward at my fork and knife.

There was a great growing void between us. I'd spent the winter hidden in a cocoon of self-loathing, drowned in cheap liquor, a prison to the four walls surrounding me in my tired, dilapidated apartment.

"Where are you?" She asked, breaking the silence that settled around our table. "I don't recognize you anymore."

The radio on the wall was bleeding out some pop-bile. "How many chords does it take for a song to vomit up real love?" I asked her. She smiled dryly.

"I don't know what to tell you. Something's changed. I've been looking for myself lately. I'm locked up by some faceless sadness, some unspeakable gloom. Maybe I should start taking my meds again." I said.

The woman came by to refill my coffee again.

"The doctor said you should stay off them, level out. You should trust his advice," She assured me.

"I don't trust anyone." I told her plainly.

"I'm going out for a cigarette." She said, offended.

Cars passed by in the night, and the dull antique moon hung in a calm hush. People went in and out through the doors, frenzied appetites, babies gasping with banshee howls. I let my mind wander to a future more comforting than the shifting, uneasy skin I sat in. I saw a great city, sprawling concrete canopy, lights flickering like candles caught in an autumn squall. A towering electric manifest to life and love and all the routines that seemed so strange to me now.

When she came back in, the wind swept up through her hair, kicking it around wild, mane-like. I was really crazy about her; deep down at the bottom of my jaded, frigid heart laid a glorious affection, smothered in time and selfishness. A left over seed desperate for illumination, a jolt of life. She was intoxicatingly beautiful, but even the most masterful sculptures can be rendered to merely somber stone through time. My own implosive behavior couldn't cater to her needs. For her, I would pack up my life, uprooted from the heart of this miserable composite of land, to look for great ease up north. I had to. Without I would drown in my self-pity, bloated with anxiety, too afraid to leave my front door. The left over rind of a life once full and feverous with passion. Hollow.

Our food was ready. Eggs, greasy and runny. I poked at the soft yolk, watching it run over the hospital white plate like a child's nose on his Sunday best. Although she said she wasn't hungry, I knew we hadn't eaten all day, and her loss of appetite was probably due to me. She hungrily devoured her hash browns, smacking her lips with sausage grease. The more we ate, the more I felt a rolling calm rinse off our dirty animosity.

I gave her a weak smile. "We're past halfway now. We might even make it there by Saturday."

"I'll call James when we're near the city. Maybe we can meet for dinner." She suggested cautiously, expecting to get a rise out of me.

"That'd be nice. Maybe Carrie will be in town as well. It's been ages since I've seen those two." I told her, watching surprise bloom across her face.

"Wow. I didn't think you'd want to she said. Hopefully she doesn't bring her asshole marine boyfriend again."

We both laughed, remembering our previous encounter. Carrie's taste in men had always supplied a plethora of hilarity and bewilderment for us.

She paid the tab while I filled up at the gas station. I watched the numbers on the pump climb upward and upward, cringing as I imagined all humanity groping for an oil teat, whining for a hideous petroleum fix. A soft hand on mine drew me to reality.

Soft lips on my cheek. Warm breath. "I'm glad we stopped." She smiled.

"I'm glad we're here." I told her and kissed her with a long forgotten desire.

"I think we'll be ok. This is only another beginning. We're still working on just living, right?" she smiled, eyes watering up.

I started the car. Headlights forward, cutting through the settled darkness. Eyes again on open road, wheels rolling onward towards starlit salvation. As the hum of the engine buzzed through my head, I was again assured that doubt was no fact, but an emotion, just as much as certainty, and they swayed on a pendulum with ferocious speed. There are some days when the sky is strangled by smog, and the trees huddle in a stale green stasis. Our words drift through empty rooms like ghosts, and love slinks like a strange animal far away in a barbwire jungle. There are also days, even moments, when we undergo a long, fresh breath of clarity and relief. When the world wide is an empty canvas, naked, to be washed over with sweet truth and bold, glaring life.

While she slept, head rested gently against the window, the radio gods blared out their gospel, and stars and satellites, gleaming lunar phosphorescence drip down from the sprawling sky. I smile, knowing that the future was wide and vast and unknown. I found solace in it, because the greatest uncertainties breed the most beautiful adventure. I plunge deep into the night, chasing the coming sun, Chicago off in the morning distance. And out at the end of the universe, sleeping in the bleak, a great light grows, like the seed in my heart, raising its eyes for coming day.

Heart Full of Hornets

Two kids died in a car accident down the road last week. It doesn't matter much to this story, but I thought I should tell you, because I thought it was quite sad.

Tell me, Brother. What's your sickness? Show your ragged bark bones, and stop talking with those tired eyes, shaky skeleton knees. Keeping things like this inside ya is like a heart full of hornets.

Are words still heavy on your tongue? Do the birds still call for you with the morning? I can see in a tired face the long lines of doubt and sorrow, rolling down high cheeks like echoes through a vacant hall. Where is your love now, Brother? Where is a sweet hand, and a soft breath? Because I can see the ailment across your eyes and scattered amongst tragic artifacts.

And do you still see with strange eyes, wonders and brilliant dreams?Where is your vision? Stifled, clotted like old blood. Brother, I have seen your best days, your longest lives. I wonder if I'll see them again.

I remember when we were young. Do you? Salty days at sun baked beaches. Fingers stained red from the summer's sweet harvest of blackberries.Liquor soaked late nights of fire smoke and laughter long into the darkness. Dionysian dreams.

When you sleep are there still auroras bursting across the vast sky in your mind? Where are your dreams, Brother? Who has laid claim to your long lost imagination. Has it drowned in despair and stale perfume? Where are your desirous and delirous days? I miss them dearly.

Do you remember her with those long streets? Silent eyes toward the day. Intimate, like whispers passing through curtained veils. You wrote to me the day she left to tell me you remembered what love felt like. What our lives sounded like when we were younger.

Can you still smell the roar of the engine? Rambling south like a broken cassette unraveling around a finger. Didn't you once tell me what freedom meant? Didn't you speak of new latitudes and rebirth?

Brother, you were given wings and roots when you left. Wings to fly towards the crest of new days, and roots to soak up the rain waters of wisdom and wonder left over from the past. Did you fly too close to the sun? Were you severed from the grounds you knew?

When I saw you last you told me that a moment worth remembering was when we found a time during the day when the world was right in front of you. When your mind drifted out of the feet you stand in and upwards towards infinity, and your hands were no longer your own but a part of everything, and the sound you drank in through your ears resonated with the universe's ancient symphonies. And you told me the immediate moment after the sobering return to reality was like realizing that you were actually happy all along.

Where is your smile now? Is it frail? Has it withered? I can tell there's something eating you alive. There must be something broken deep beneath that flesh machine. It pains me to see you like this.

On the night you left we sailed candles out into the pond in celebration of chapters closing. Who is writing your book now? Hang onto the pen for dear life, Brother.

I'll write your weary soul a prescription and sell your sins to the gutters, because I've got every screw to yr dismantled spirit. Tell me what to do to mend your broken bones and heal the holes in your head and heart. There is a hand outstretched for you, Brother, and God Dammit, it will ruin you and I both if you are too lost to take it.

This morning I went to the funeral of the two kids. I cried and mourned. Their death was tragic, but what truly resonated was realizing the glaring death swarming around the memory of my dear friend. This is my last plea. Don't lose sight of life and love, Brother, because that is all anyone has left. Take two of these, one as you wake up and one at night. And if you are able to raise your head to the new day's light the next morning, to shake off the old dust settled around your tattered carapace, I will be singing your name out in the streets. Arms open. Waiting.

Storm Internal

I watched Stephen pick up the broken glass from the floor and make five precise cuts on the top of his hand. He didn't flinch as the blood poured out. Tears were already falling from his eyes, and his pacing footsteps continued to fill the otherwise silent garage.

I winced at the blood. Blood, red like mine, violent red, red as the once living leaves, now dead on the wet ground outside. I grimaced at the self-mutilation, the destruction of a dear friend's mind and body. I searched desperately for words, any sort of advice of justification, a way to rationalize those deep unsettling moments.

Stephen told me, plainly and bluntly, that there was no point in caring about anything, because it all led to loss. That as much as anyone could convince themselves that they had filled their lives with good, it was all a sick artifice. I blurted out that sometimes there was gold in shit, it's just harder to find. That the best times could arise out of the worst. He looked back to me, finally distracted from his torrent pacing and affirmed that shit is only shit.

For someone who cares so much about words, I am surprised how often I don't have anything to say. And on this particular morning, watching this particular friend bleed those particular drops of blood onto our garage floor, my tongue sat motionless in arrest. I wondered, how do I convince someone that there are things to believe in, when they are staring in your face, telling you that love is a lie?

This got me all riled up. Love is a lie? It doesn't exist? Then what is any of this all about? I retraced my mental steps back to the previous spring, when he told me he met a beautiful girl. A girl who made him nervous, who made him go into Mi Piace and buy a cup of coffee everyday just to see her. A girl who smoked, which made him put his cigarettes on the table next to his lattes just so she might ask him to join her outside. I followed these thoughts to summertime, where I watched from the stage and the port, singing songs about the loves I'd lost and found, while they sat and listened together, eyes buzzing with nervous joy at the notion of sharing the moment together. I thought of the summer in Sweden, he and I fresh off the plane, my ears full of swooning and musings about his beautiful Heidi, and despite how beautiful all those tall, blonde Scandinavians running around with us were, he was only interested in his island girl. His dedication, vindicating the notion that the heart's song was not continent bound.

Love has always been a fleeting phantom in my life. As soon as it appears, it is gone, and I've accepted the fact that in romance, my romantic life is only a series of exits and entrances. However, Stephen made me believe in it again. His emotion was so pure and I could see it in scribbled between the lines of his words and movements that he was head over heels, crazy. Crazy enough to move to Olympia with her. Committing to the fantastic experiment of young and relentless love. Compromising sanity and space. Willing and indentured to the turbulence of fortune. Celebrating the most powerful act of the human heart, to try. Open to the possibility of utter collapse, but poised for the soul's garden to flourish at the hands of another. I was riddled with admiration. They reassured me that anyone could fall off the deep ends of desire and find home in another. That despite my jaded and bitter heart, there were other flames burning, that the fireworks of a beautiful smile could light up the skies residing within me.

Here was Stephen, a wreck before me. Telling me that me that nothing would be all right because he was not a resident of Olympia, but of his relationship. Heidi was his home and his heart and his city surrounding him, and he couldn't bare the fact that its foundation was crumbling before him.

I started to understand the way he was feeling. When you are a stranger to the city you live in, and the closest thing you have to home has turned it's back, you are all alone. I told him that he had his friends and his family, but none of those things could offer any comfort. I joked that this was the sort of thing that happened when you gamble a relationship on a yearlong lease. It has to work, because you're legally obligated to live together. He smiled and told me that he knew.

Stephen left the house after he had calmed down. He didn't know when he was going to be back. By then I would have guessed that he might be going as far away as possible. Seattle, San Juan, Canada, I had no idea. I went outside for cigarette after cigarette.

By the time the sun had gone down I had worked myself into a big frenzy. My life here in Olympia had become too turbulent. The weight of my roommates' collective problems was heavy on my mind. I was now the one pacing around the house.

The creaking sound of an opening door jarred me from my computer, and I breathed a sigh of relief to see Stephen and Heidi strolling in through the hallway, looking reasonably content. The kitchen filled with smells of dinner and whispers of forgiveness. Peace had finally settled upon all our weary hides.

It is a violent act on the soul to pit oneself against the madness that emerges from life in Olympia. I have fallen causality many times. Dark clouds may drift over the west side, but Stephen and Heidi are learning to find the breaks in the clouds here. They know how to find warmth in this city's cold arms, because they have built community in one another. Their love is as wild as the storms perched above the Sound, but I'm no meteorologist, and I, like them find comfort in the hard rains of confusion and frustration, because every war has an armistice and in fights we find forgiveness.

Lost Continents

This was the sort of place that sent us on hunts for lost continents or mansions veiled behind vine trellises. The slums of a caustic nowhere. Like dead tealeaves n a beggar's cup.

The windows were all blown out, spanning buildings in rows like lines of bad coke. Each one creased with aged moss and dirt, and soot congregated along the tarnished sills. Long streaks of rain and bird shit inhabited the cracked panes that delivered a view inside or out that was both unavailable and undesirable.

The base of the buildings bled out water like sweat cascading down the feet of an overweight man in the sauna. These old buildings shared no kinship with anything human: big tanks of liquid, organs, and skin. No, in these guts, only brick and scrap metal lined intestinal walls. We both shared the same foundation though, grasping at damp ground, drifting through the pools of Monday's sour downpour, the dark runoff of a cloud's tantrum up high.

The streets, cobbled and zigzagged, running up and down the city's spine like accordion folds, were paled with poverty and remorse.I moved through them, cold with the emptiness of the outskirt shanties. I stepped carefully through the graceless pavement.

Down below the spire towers, perched up like owls' nests on the hill above the city, was a great river – I say great only to emphasize it's immensity, but remain firm in my pleas for it's illness. Old fish heads bobbed in and out of the wake, while sick bubbles belched out of rusted, skeletal piping.

I motioned along a carcass of a boulevard, scouring for life. Shadows of boney crows flicked through the streets, warbling overhead. I kept going, moving through the alleyways, searching for signs of humanity. It was definitively around; fresh garbage littered the street, footprints in the collected soot, cigarettes still burning at the mouths of sewers. I followed the long shadows of some form of crooked existence slanting outside a warehouse. Footsteps quickening, I hurried after, unsure of what may be waiting for me in this particular soul and visage, but pacing deliberately, still. Around the corner to reveal that it was an elderly man. His coat was old and moth eaten, beard long and unkempt – the graying image of Dean Morriarty, perhaps – emitting the general stench of piss and loneliness. I didn't want to give myself away so I stepped quietly at a distance.

I can't place specifically what signaled my advances, but the man wheeled around abruptly, ever aware of my impending presence and persistence. He stepped towards me in a wake of strange fury and surprise. I wanted to back away, into the cracks and holes of the battered street, but I remained stuck in arrest.He grabbed me by the lapel, giving me eyes of the electric chair.Mouth cracked open, exposing teeth like jagged Himalayan ranges, breath like sick cod. He wound his expression up tight, searching for words. With eyes hard into mine he asked, " What does a stranger find in a city that hides its eyes in the black gutters of loneliness, frozen in an hourless hush? A city, whose tailored petticoats have long tarnished in the furrow of fortune's fist. Lungs of a great gasping machine, hiccupping in the cosmic smog. The old seraphim souls wandering out from wild hives to shave their beards and pander for cheap talk. We are shorelined – shipwrecked, even – in the disparity of it. " I was wandering in the immensity of his cadence, his deliberateness and calloused diction. He continued still.

"The angels' wings have all pixilated against the sky's cold horizons. The only banners of hope to hold high anymore are scribbled out in dead languages and flap frailly in the naked breeze. The whispers of the inhabitants are lured out in coughing fits, caught by the cobwebs of corrosion that catch and claw, like the many Shivan arms that plucked the fruits of metropolis' bending boughs, giving way to stark sprouts and stocks in the urban orchard, incarcerated in boundless winter," pausing, and then to me again, "So where do we find our Paradise? "

The man inquired further, rational grounded parallel to the same improbability as the explanations of sunken cities of legends lost, the same disgust as someone who trips and falls into realizations of the horrors in symmetry, with the decisiveness of a man who seeks to rely on faith to turn fiction into fact. The same surrealism of the believers who tried to lend us their madness just to see the sun-spotted face of young Christ – or Buddha, or Mary the mother, even – "No one gives the mom's any credit anymore," I laughed to myself.

I couldn't pry him off if I tried. Shake as I might, his grip was ironclad and his resolve was as steely as the factory garters casing the neighborhood streets. Out from his mouth rambled a soliloquy of broken dreams, burials of slanted language, "The genie's lamp has rattled, but long silenced. I just want three wishes these days," he continued. "There was once a city that thrived with the life of brilliant suns, that ran with pristine machinery – dynamos of electric, thriving subsistence. Who's days questioned death with equivalent zeal as the explorers that lusted after whispers of Atlantis, or the mathematicians that tried to apply reason to the algebra of the universe's antique opus. We see curvature in the paths to utopia here, because we are hard pressed to squint through the pestilence of defeat," – he steamrolled along – "My first wish," he declared, "is to not occupy the tombs of remorse any more, to cast away the shackles of these hard-trodden streets. There is a love to be found here, it's just buried under rubble."

I scoured the surrounding streets wondering if love had ever coursed through their sick veins, what hellish scorn had driven it away?

"My second wish," He went on, "for you to know the city that was before, as I knew it – the city that nurtured me from womb, and raised me up to walk amongst skyscrapers, burgeoning with growth and promise," waving towards the hideous conurbation's bones. "And my last wish is to take you to the lungs of this once great city's last gasping breath."

I paused at his request.

"Unlike the heart and body, which suffers inside out, blackening at the core, we've seen cancerous urban decay close in upon us like locust swarms. Stripped of pristine beauty and life by war and famine, myriad catastrophe, as if the gods were dogged to cleave us from the very earth we call home. But the fray is fiery, because home is worth fighting for. Home is all we have."

I grimaced at the notion, heart weighing heavy amongst the depressed ruins. I had run across the country looking for it's voice, and had only found the horse croak of this weeping metropolis. Hailing from nowhere, a perpetual tourist. looking for anyplace with warm bed and hooks to hang hats and coats. I was off balance again in my unfastening anguish. The man, however, remained unflinchingly rigid in his supplications.

He told me that he wore his battered soul like a badge, speaking of a city that could be, that failed to exist in space in time, but preserved in hearts and minds of masses, hand in hand. That everyone here was hard pressed for better days, and looking for something to ease the weight of urban atrophy. That despite the splinters in the city's shell to roll over on behalf of its withered condition was to throw in the towel on not only yourself, but all its inhabitants.

The man asked me to come with him. I obliged.

Through fragile streets, along dark corridors of unruly concrete and battered, twisted metal, he took me towards the city's gasping center. The buildings. though taller and less desolate showed no signs of prosperity or improvement. Still, broken and thrashed wreckage littered the roads, while the trees halted in a scorched immobility, like burnt matchsticks lining the sidewalks. Further, the buildings cast shadows over us from the low yolky sun, dripping down across the sky like a runny nose. The grey buildings crawled with vines, like burst capillaries spanning the architecture, upward towards the last slivers of light.

A sudden shift in aesthetics swept through the concrete canopy as we walked toward the city's core. At the center there was an opening, dense with foliage, greener than all the eyes of loves lost. The contrast was harsh, and my brain was swollen by this sudden oasis' majesty.

The scarred urban landscape had given way to lush and endless green. The city opened up like parting lips, giving way to vital origin.Lucid pools of crystal water speckled the verdant haven, while the lotuses and swallows bobbed in the settling evening mist. I stood captive in bewilderment.

As my eyes stood vigilant to the open field, now moving with people young and old, ears drinking in the first sounds of laughter and real joy, my heart felt it's first organic stirrings and elation froth to the surface of memory's deep ocean. A hand on my shoulder was like soft music. The old man smiled with delight at my sudden euphoria.

People were gathered, sharing bread and beams to one another with unfathomable accord. Young children, proof of this city's fertility, ran about, playing, singing through thriving plots of corn, tomatoes, basil, and turnips. There was music even, a slow nocturne. A requiem perhaps? This hunch was affirmed, as I looked beyond the garden to see graves surrounding the clearing, artifacts of the warring epoch, memoirs the city's former dynamism.

The man handed me bread and wine appending to the moment's serenity and splendor. "Rest well weary traveler. I welcome you to sanctuary. It brings me great pride to show you the beating heart of our sick metropolis. And I assure you that it is beating, kicking even, despite it's wounded vessel."

"But how can you have hope for such condition, such looming ailment?"

"There is no cure for cancer and we, as much as anyone else, are servants to cruel impermanence. Our home suffers with injury and misfortune, but this refuge is a manifestation of human spirit clamoring for our willing and dutiful servitude. All is not lost yet, for we have endured the pangs and arrows of a disdainful fate, and with knowing and determined acceptance we press onward. An oak does not start without seed, and though time, ike those of the sub-atomic, has smashed around us in wild, random, sometimes unforgiving chaos, without it we do not have energy, energy to climb the tall mountains before us towards recovery and deliverance. We are the medicine coursing through this city's festering blood, and we will clutch its fragile frame until our final expiration, or the city itself draws us down with it to the jaws of hell. So we entreat on another to root firmly and grow tall and mighty together."

I sat with my wine, letting it run through me, finding anchorage in the port of another's humanity and the grandeur the soul's collective will.

Dearest Isabella

Dearest Isabella,

   This is the truth for the first time in as long as I can remember. The whole truth. The deliberate truth.

   Some time has passed since I've last seen you; glowing in the spring sun, wind through your long dress, eyes forward toward the water, hiding a soft sadness. Chatter floating through the portside market, buses coming and going, soon to return me to a reality far from the dream like days we experienced together. I was choking on the bitter-sweetness of all of it while you talked with a friend about something, wondering if the beauty I had seen in the last three days would ever come my way again, if you and I were destined to be merely a memory to be kept away and cherished, eventually antiquated and fossilized beneath layers of life and love and loss to follow.

   You kissed me before I left and told me that it had been strange and beautiful together. When you walked away, back into the city streets, I wondered if you were crying. I wondered what it all meant to you. I still haven't come to a conclusion that I can settle with. Because whether I tell myself that it meant anything to you, doubt or dreams continue to beg the contrary.

That was the longest bus ride I ever took. I remember sitting at the curb in Sacramento, smoking one of the cigarettes that you reluctantly bought me, and looking back on the last two years of my life. I was almost furious with myself. How I had allowed you to sneak into my heart and grab hold with unshakeable vigor. I spent the fall after I met you in and out of Seattle, trying to just see you. Just to hear your voice. Just to see your smile. I bent over backwards because I knew that it was worth it, and that though we were freshly acquainted then, I was and would always be at my best when I was with you.

Months would pass eventually, and all you would be was a voice on the other line or a name dancing in the back of my mind. But when I saw you, at times that seemed almost miraculous coincidental crossings of our paths, my heart sped up and my words got all mixed, and I knew that you were absolutely incredible.

It's hard to say, whether or not we would even recognize each other now. I have been at the mercy of my inescapably hectic routines for some time now. And you are off, swimming out in all that thick, vivid life. That is to say, forever in motion, while I, for the first time in as long as I can remember, have hit a snag of nauseating stillness. It's as though the planets are aligned more often that we are.

But since I last saw you I have had the most valuable commodity at my hands: indefinite and invaluable time. Time to think, time to breath, time for silence, time for sadness, time to dream, and time to distract myself from my own looming madness. In my time I have affirmed things about life that have kept the day long, and music beautiful, and strawberries sweet, and the smell of low tide crisp and salty.

This is what I know now.

I trust you, because I know what your hands look like. I know that your fingers are short and skinny, and always cold because you don't have enough iron in your blood. I know that you have a long, deeply engraved lifeline running down your palm, while mine is short and thin, which always worried you. I know that your hand looks good with mine, and sometimes gets a little sweaty. Your fingers are decorated in rings, watch on the wrist. I know that you told me that if you had to give up one of your senses, you swore that you could never lose touch, because otherwise we would grope our way through reality, like a blind man reaches for his canned soup. We needed our hands to hold onto our sanity and to one another.

I know that I want you, and probably will for a long time to come, maybe always. When I hear sweet music or drink champagne, or walk through Capital Hill and down Valencia Street in San Francisco, or take a long drive or read a thick novel, I will somehow find myself running down the roads of my memories of the time we shared together. I can start anywhere, but my heart keeps guiding my thoughts back to you. Ushering me back to the feeling of being completely overwhelmed, completely crazy, panicked and anxious, but most poignantly, utterly helpless to your gentile and sweet ways.

I know that I will never have you now, and that you are a bright star, bursting across this universe. A heart set alight like a bouquet of lanterns. Glowing with radiant life, eyes saturated with glistening and insatiable desire for everything all of the time. I can be certain that there is solace in that fact, and undeniable comfort in your assured victorious and triumphs through life, I will be sorely remiss to have only been granted a brief peer through the window of a dreamer's dream.

On the night I returned home, the first time in six months, I found myself saying hello to a friend who'd I'd last seen nearly an entire continent away from the small ferry we rode, bound for a microscopic island bordering Victoria, BC, late on a May evening. I remember waving goodbye to this wandering soul, as he sped off in a rented car along the Costa Rican highways. Out of San Jose towards Vulcan Arenal, with a girl he'd met three days prior in a mojito-fueled madness on the Caribbean coast.

We were jubilant and severely duped by the sheer brilliance of fate. Decidedly agreeing that if it wasn't at one another's funeral, the only logical place we could've met was a ferry, island bound.

We laughed and regaled each other with stories from time apart. He told me of the alien, fraternal desert tribes of WSU, soaked in beer and sorority sweat. The sound of the sickening machine-like assembly of drones, suburban cowboys, cheap fraternal brotherhood, and geographically confused bohemians and hipsters. He battled my distaste with equal blows towards my school, asking where my dreadlocks were, and what grade I was getting in 'Feelings Class.'

"Oh wait. You don't even have grades," he laughed while I hid behind my cigarette in embarrassment.

We laughed about how our state as human beings had deteriorated entirely while traveling together in the tropics. Recounting one of the last evenings together, in which an overjoyed Egyptian man insisted we celebrated his birthday with him, providing us with beer and falafel in exchange that we learn to belly dance. Our friend and designated wet blanket of the trip, Andrew refused to participate, but somehow ended up with a handle of vodka and a plate of handmade hummus and pita bread. And the night fell into a spell of bizarre celebration as our new friend, Ali Baba showered us in drink, Arabic song and dance, and even brought out a velvet cape, that with he tried to cover our fellow traveler Ali (also once nicknamed 'Ali Baba') and kiss her on the dance floor.

We smiled with our fond memories and the sheer magic our fated meeting. We rode in silence, smoking, sharing the only beer in his backpack on the bow of the ferry, to not be seen by the people driving the boat. I told him that I went to San Francisco for a week.

He smiled and said, "Thank God."

As much as his and my coincidental meeting had taken me by surprise, caught me off guard, it's serendipitous nature ran alarmingly parallel to our long and storied history of coincidence and improbability. The pages of our chronology are soaked with the random and fateful shifting of time and the great ebbing fow of the universe. Narrated in chaotic and beautiful prose, that resonates through the deepest caverns of the soul.

I had flown into Seattle in the evening, and you were seeing Devendra Banhart at the Showbox. I was there, smoking, on my phone, and you were beautiful, drenched in the afterglow of music and sweat and dancing. The words we shared down near First and Pike meant everything to me then.

You said we needed to talk and I was ready to listen. You kissed me there, in the middle of the dark street and told me to come to see you. I promised I would and we would be in the same place at the same time for the first time, just to know, some bizarre romantic experiment to d scover one another. I was terrified.

I left the next morning, borrowing ten dollars from my uncle to take the bus back to Olympia, unsure of what was to come.

I made it home early, off balance, feeling like a stranger, feeling frustrated that you were once again far away, and all the sweet words we shared could have been only ghostly whispers that would replay in my mind; dull and distant.

I went to a party that night. Drinking to slow my restless mind. People were excited to see me. I had been gone a long time, and I didn't care much to say goodbye when I left. They didn't remember, and their warmth was a pleasant distraction.

I wandered aimlessly through the smoky crowd of people. There was music inside, but I just wanted it to be quiet. My friend made small talk, and I told him about the jungle. We were all on spring break then, and no one wanted to stay in town.

"I'm going to San Francisco tomorrow," he told me.

Suddenly the night came into focus, and all the noise I was trying to tune out had faded into insignificance.

"Do you have room?" I asked hopefully.

"It's just me and Gabee. I don't see why not," he smiled.

We made arrangements for the next morning, and suddenly the magic from the city streets coursed through me again. I called you before I left the party. Neither of us could believe it. You didn't want me to show up till Thursday, because your mom was in town, and I took that as a good sign, because it led me to believe that our time together might not have been mom appropriate.

I smoked a joint on the walk home to ensure a good night's rest, because otherwise I would have writhed in anticipation, sleepless.

And then I was out of Olympia, on the road once again. A day and a half of passing scenery led me across that bright red bridge and into your arms and the rest blurred into beautiful oblivion.

You are far away from me again, and I think you will be for some time. However, these words are permanent, and I stand by them, like you stood by me waiting for the greyhound. For the first time I am glad to have you far away, because with each day you grow less and less tangible, and turn slowly into an idea more than a person, who once completely consumed my thoughts. A notion like that makes me feel as comfortable as I was wrapped up in your soft arms in the early morning hours.

I used to dream about seeing you again far later in our lives. We both had aged, but you were still so graceful. We ate and drank and watched the birds fly away from the city square where we met.

Isabella, this may find you at a strange time or in a beautiful place, but know that comes from a sound mind and a healthy heart. I am fine, I promise. I miss you madly, and wish you well. Know that my love for you is strong and reaches far across the Atlantic with these words. I don't know when I will see you next, but I assure you that it will be magnificent. If you get distracted from the velocity of your fantastic life, and ever miss me, know that I am sprawled all over these pages and through our favorite songs. Until then, good luck sweet traveler, my smile is with you.

Yours,

Lee

Andy Sontag

Avery Adams

I am inspired by what is beautiful - its creation and how it can best be captured. Flashing lights, and the click of the shutter are the beating of my heart. I attended the Photographic Center Northwest in Seattle before coming to Olympia. I live to collaborate with other artist, bridging our difference to create something unique and original. Hailing from quaint and creative Yellow Springs OH, I have been raised with creativity and aesthetic beauty.

I would like to extend a thank you to my heros, my parents and friends.

I feel constantly fortunate and frustrated with my need to externalize the world on the page. Born to an artist and a musician, I really had no choice but to create, and found myself playing the part of the writer for as long as I can remember. It has become a consuming passion that I take great pride in, and conversely see no other way that I could deal with the world around me. I studied at the Evergreen State College with a focus in Creative Writing. My short story 'Lost Continents' was published in Slightly West Literary Magazine, and won first prize for Adult Prose-Fiction in San Juan County with the story 'Exoskeletal.' I currently find residence in Olympia, WA.

I would like to thank Mom and Dad for roots and wings, Sharon Lannan, Shelle Cropper, Joanna Brodziak, and Wynn Barnard for diligent ed ting, my beautiful friends who constantly inspire, San Juan Island for the challenges and triumphs it has provided me, and my good time gal, Olympia, WA, of which without it's madness, none of this would have been possible.

www.ingramcontent.com/pod-product-compliance
Lightning Source LLC
Chambersburg PA
CBHW041349010726
47507CB00002B/104